*Crazy . . . ?*

"You have to break up with her," Shannon said, raising her head slowly. Her eyes were red-rimmed, as if she'd been crying. Her hair was more tangled than usual, one twisted strand falling down over an eye.

"What? Are you crazy?"

She didn't react to him at all, didn't even look at him. "You have to break up with her," she repeated in a low, steady voice.

"You're *my* baby now."

*point*

# THE GIRLFRIEND

*R.L. Stine*

SCHOLASTIC INC.
New York Toronto London Auckland Sydney

ISBN 0-590-44333-X

12 11 10 9 8 7 6 5 4                    2 3 4 5 6/9

Printed in the U.S.A.                    01

First Scholastic printing, December 1991

# THE GIRLFRIEND

# Chapter 1

"I'd like to propose a toast to Scotty and Lora," Mr. DeMarco announced. He raised his fluted champagne glass above his head and held it there until the large, crowded room grew quiet.

Scotty tried to hide behind Lora, but she turned and pulled him beside her, her expression playfully scolding. "This is embarrassing," Scotty whispered.

"Get used to it," Lora told him, holding him in place with both hands so he couldn't escape. "My dad *loves* embarrassing people. It's his hobby."

"I know, I know," Scotty replied, shaking his head, his eyes on the front of the large rec room where Lora's dad was still holding his champagne glass in the air, waiting for all the guests to raise their glasses.

Scotty and Lora had been a couple since sixth grade, so Scotty knew exactly what to expect from her parents. Both of them were warm, and outgoing, and generous. Too generous, Scotty sometimes thought.

They smother you with kindness. That's how he sometimes described them.

Scotty felt smothered by this lavish party, with the enormous, seemingly endless buffet table, the overstocked bar, the five-piece band out on the terrace, the young waiters parading around in their black tuxedos, carrying silver trays of salmon and caviar hors d'oeuvres.

After all, it was a little too early to celebrate.

Scotty and Lora had received preliminary acceptance at Princeton, but nothing official yet. And Scotty might not be able to go anyway. He was still waiting to hear about his scholarship.

Scotty and Lora had urged the DeMarcos to wait a while before having the party. For one thing, it was only November. They still had the rest of their senior year at Glenview High to finish.

But, Mr. DeMarco, in typical fashion, had insisted on throwing this huge, expensive party. "Don't worry about it," he had said, his youthful face beaming happily, one big arm around each of them, crushing them both in an affectionate hug. "We'll throw another party after the school year. Or maybe *two* parties — one for each of you!"

Scotty and Lora finally gave up trying to discourage him. "What's the point?" Lora asked, as they were sitting in the front seat of her father's BMW, parked up by Rainer Point, overlooking the town. "Daddy will always be Daddy."

"But it's so bogus!" Scotty exclaimed unhappily.

"I mean, throwing a party for us for no reason."

"I wish you wouldn't say 'bogus' all the time," Lora said, squeezing his hand affectionately. "I mean, we're going to Princeton, you know — not Ohio State."

They both laughed.

"You're a stuck-up snob," Scotty said.

"And you love it," she replied and kissed him for a long time.

Scotty did love it, he had to admit. He liked everything about Lora. He liked how her wavy, blonde hair caught the sunlight, how soft it felt in his hands. He liked staring into her wide, green eyes. He liked the way people said she looked like a model, like a young Christie Brinkley.

He liked walking down the hall at school with her, holding hands. "You know we're a cliché," he'd tell her. "I mean, the football quarterback and the Homecoming Queen? Get real!"

"I don't feel like a cliché," she'd reply in her serious way. "I just feel like me."

He had to admit he didn't at all mind that they were a cliché. Being with Lora always made him feel good. And he was proud of being the starting quarterback of the Tigers. He'd been voted all-state last year in his junior year. That was pretty good.

Scotty liked the fact that everyone thought of him and Lora as a couple. And he liked the fact that other kids were jealous of them. And of him. He didn't think about it a lot, but when he did, he admitted to himself that having this long, steady relationship with one girl was maybe the most admirable thing about him.

Other kids, even his best friends, even Bender, his very best friend, seemed sort of aimless to him. Immature.

Scotty like being responsible. Maybe it was because his father had been so irresponsible. Running off without a word, leaving Mrs. Singleton to bring up Scotty and his younger brother Denny.

How could he *do* that to us? Scotty often asked himself.

He never came up with a satisfactory answer.

Lora's parents seemed to have such a close, stable relationship. Maybe that was why Scotty liked them so much.

He realized he liked being with the DeMarcos as much as with his own family. When he didn't feel smothered by their wealth, by their enthusiasm, by their generosity.

Now he found himself looking around the large, brightly lit rec room, crowded with kids from school, relatives of both families, and a lot of people he'd never seen before, and *definitely* feeling smothered.

"We never should have agreed to this," he whispered, leaning against Lora.

"We had no choice, remember?" she whispered back, as her father rambled on with one of his endless, meandering toasts.

"But it's so embarrassing," Scotty moaned, staring across the room at his friend Bender, who was leaning against one of the sliding glass doors, staring back at Scotty with his eyes crossed and his tongue hanging out of his mouth.

"Don't think of it as a going to Princeton party. Think of it as a going-away party for me," Lora said, playfully stepping down hard on his foot until he winced in pain, her eyes straight ahead as if concentrating on her father's toast.

Scotty was tempted to pour his Coke down the front of her green velvet party dress, but managed to hold himself back.

He had almost forgotten that Lora and her parents were going away. Off to London and Paris for a week. Mr. DeMarco had some sort of architectural business to take care of in London, so why not turn it into a spur-of-the-moment family vacation?

He glanced at his mother, in her flowing fuchsia-and-electric-blue dress, which was just a little too snug on her plump body, her platinum hair piled high on her head, standing in front of Mr. DeMarco, glass in hand, listening so intently.

For a brief moment, Scotty felt real envy. He wanted to be in the DeMarco family. He wanted to go on unplanned trips to Europe, too.

Oh, well, some day soon, I *will* be a member of the family, he thought, glancing affectionately at Lora.

". . . I'm real proud of these kids . . ." Mr.

DeMarco was saying at the front of the room.

And then Mrs. DeMarco looked away from her husband and gasped.

Mr. DeMarco stopped abruptly in mid-sentence. All eyes turned to where his wife was staring — to the buffet table, where Fluffernutter, Lora's little white cat, had leaped up and was enthusiastically sampling a good helping of the salmon mousse.

"Oh, Fluffernutter!" Lora cried, letting go of Scotty's hand and rushing toward the buffet table.

One of the tuxedoed waiters got there first and lifted the still-chewing cat off the table, setting it gently down on the linoleum floor.

"I think that was a sign that I've been talking too long," Mr. DeMarco said, grinning. He held up his glass one more time. "To Scotty and Lora," he announced, looking for Lora. He couldn't see her because she was down on the floor scolding her cat.

There was a clinking of glasses, and conversations resumed around the room. Scotty breathed a loud sigh of relief, took a long gulp of Coke from his glass, and started over to thank Lora's dad for the toast, even though he hadn't really heard much of it.

"Hey, man," Bender caught his arm. "Watch out for those caviar thingies. I tried one, but it tasted real fishy."

"I'll be careful," Scotty said dryly.

Bender was tall and lanky, the tallest one in the room even though he was only seventeen, and still growing. He should've played basketball, Scotty thought. He never could figure out why his friend wanted to be an offensive tackle.

"What kind of a party is this without any pizza?" Bender complained, only half serious.

"It wasn't *my* idea, man," Scotty said, sighing. "You want to go out for a pizza? I'll go with you."

"Yeah. Sure," Bender said sarcastically, glancing down at Lora who was still on the floor playing with Fluffernutter, unaware that she was getting white cat hair all over her green velvet dress. "You ready for Friday night?"

Scotty nodded. What with all the excitement over being accepted at Princeton and the party, he hadn't had much time to think about the game. "Lincoln isn't that good," he said.

"They're five-and-oh!" Bender exclaimed, pushing his heavy, black-plastic Buddy Holly eyeglasses up on his narrow nose. "They beat Westerville 35 to zip, and we could only tie Westerville."

"They got lucky, man," Scotty said, grinning. "They're bogus. Totally bogus. We can take 'em."

He saw Mr. DeMarco coming toward him, so he slapped Bender's hand in a low five and started to push his way through the crowd to meet him.

Mr. DeMarco, chewing a fried chicken finger, beamed at Scotty, raking back his thick, brown hair with one hand. He's so proud of his hair, Scotty thought. He's always telling everyone how he's forty-five and still has every hair he ever had.

"Hey, thanks for the toast," Scotty said, trying to sound enthusiastic.

Mr. DeMarco brushed chicken crumbs from his wide red tie. "I think I went on a bit too long, but I just couldn't help it." He flung an arm around Scotty's shoulder, nearly knocking Scotty over. "I'm just so proud of you two!"

"Thanks," Scotty said uncomfortably.

"You know, I have a little bet on the game Friday night," he said confidentially, his arm still around Scotty's shoulders, guiding him toward the hallway that led to the rest of the house.

"You're betting on Lincoln?" Scotty joked.

Mr. DeMarco stopped for a moment, then laughed. "No way," he said. "You're going to be all-state again this year, Scotty. And you're going to take the Tigers to the state championship. I know it."

"Well . . . I don't know," Scotty said, feeling his face grow hot. "We've got some tough games. And with Jergens hurt . . ."

"You just have to throw more," Mr. DeMarco said. It was one of his steady themes. Scotty was too generous, he was always saying. Scotty should forget about sharing the glory. He should throw the ball more. The team should ride on Scotty's arm.

"I don't think Coach Hawkins would agree," Scotty always replied.

"Who *cares* about Hawkins?" was Mr. DeMarco's answer. "He's a chemistry teacher. What does *he* know about football?"

Scotty never won this argument. He seldom won any argument against Lora's father. Mr. DeMarco was too powerful and too insistent. He never gave up until he got his way.

"Listen, Scotty, I meant everything I said in that toast," he said, turning serious, his face close to Scotty's. "Keep making me proud, son. I know you will. I know you and Lora both will. Keep making me proud. You know, when you graduate from Princeton in four years, there'll be a place waiting for you in my firm."

Scotty's mouth dropped open in surprise. "Really?"

It was quite a generous offer. Mr. DeMarco's architectural design firm was the biggest in the state and was rapidly getting a national reputation.

Scotty planned to go into architecture at Princeton. His dream was to build amazing skyscrapers, to change skylines. Now it looked as if his dream would most certainly come true.

"Thank you, Mr. DeMarco. That's just awesome," he exclaimed. "I really don't know what to say."

Mr. DeMarco was looking past Scotty, back into the room. The glass doors had been opened. Outside, the band had started to play, and people were drifting out onto the large, flagstone terrace to dance. "I can't believe what a beautiful evening we got," he said to Scotty. "Imagine? Sixty-five degrees in November? It's like spring out there. Luck just seems to rain down on you and Lora."

"I guess so," Scotty said, still thinking about Mr. DeMarco's amazing offer. He said good-bye to him and headed excitedly over to Lora, who was talking animatedly, circled by friends from school.

It took Scotty a while to separate her from the group. Then he led her out onto the terrace, which was lit by pale pink light from paper lanterns strung around the sides.

"If all the leaves weren't down, I'd think it was summer," Lora said, taking a deep breath of the fresh, cool air. "What were you and my dad talking about?"

Scotty couldn't hold in the news a second longer. He told Lora about her father's job offer.

"That's so exciting!" Lora cried. She kissed him enthusiastically.

Walking with his arm around her shoulder, he led her across the crowded terrace. The swimming pool was drained and covered with its winter canvas tarp. He led her past it, past the small pool house and into the large, sloping backyard, away from the lights and the music. They stepped over the wet grass, walking around the carefully trimmed evergreens and shrubs.

"I shouldn't have complained," he said softly. "It's turned out to be a great party. Totally awesome."

"I think Fluffernutter stole the show," Lora said, snuggling against him.

"Fluffernutter stole the salmon," he corrected her. "I should've brought *my* pet. That would liven up the party."

"Your snake?" She made a disgusted face. "Yuck."

He pretended to be hurt, as he always did when she insulted his snake. "I think Ernie is cute," he teased.

Lora started to say something — but only managed a choked gasp as a dark figure, arms raised to attack, leaped out at them from behind a tall bush.

# Chapter 2

Scotty threw his arms up as the dark figure lunged at him, wrapping him in a tight bear hug.

"Denny!" Scotty yelped. "Are you *nuts*?!"

"You scared me to death!" Lora cried, holding her hand up to her thudding heart.

Scotty's seven-year-old brother let go of Scotty, tossed his head back, and laughed. "Gotcha!"

"You got us, all right," Scotty agreed, still feeling the effects of the shock. He reached forward and picked Denny up off the ground.

"Hey — put me down!" Denny protested, still laughing.

But Scotty held his brother up over his head like a pair of weights and began to twirl him easily.

"Put me down! I'll puke on you!" Denny

screamed. "I had a big dinner, Scotty! I'll puke on you!"

Scotty quickly returned his brother to the ground.

"Hey — you're strong," Denny admitted grudgingly.

"You're a featherweight," Scotty said, straightening his necktie and sports jacket.

It was true. Scotty and Denny didn't look at all like brothers. Denny was short and slender. Scotty was tall, broad-chested, with a thick football player's neck, muscular arms, and big hands. Denny had curly black hair that he wanted kept cut very short because he didn't like it to be curly; small, dark eyes; and delicate features. Scotty had straight, light brown hair that he kept short on top but down to his collar in the back, big blue eyes, and a large nose that looked as if it had been broken even though it hadn't. Denny always looked serious. Scotty seldom did.

"What were you doing behind that bush?" Lora demanded, holding Denny in place by pressing both hands against his shoulders.

"Hiding," he said.

"Hiding? Why?" Lora asked, not letting him go, even though he was trying desperately to squirm away.

"To scare somebody. It's a party, right?"

Lora laughed. Denny scampered back out of her grasp.

"Denny knows how to party," Scotty exclaimed,

putting his arm around Lora's shoulder. She shivered. There was a chill in the air. "It's a party, so you scare someone."

"What *else* is there to do, stupid?" Denny asked, sneering.

"You don't have to call names," Scotty said, frowning.

"Well, you're stupid," Denny repeated. He said the word a few more times. It was his favorite word. He said it all day long.

"Why don't you go inside and play in the sour cream dip?" Lora suggested.

"You're stupid, too," Denny told her. He turned and ran back toward the terrace. "I'm going to tell Mom you two were kissing and stuff!" he yelled before disappearing into the crowd.

"He's real cute," Scotty said sarcastically.

"He *is* kind of cute," Lora said, nestling her head against his shoulder. He smelled her hair. It smelled of coconut.

"He's a shrimp," Scotty muttered. "He'll never make the team."

Mentioning the team made him think of the game against Lincoln the following Friday night. "I can't believe you're missing Homecoming," he said, not meaning to whine.

"I know. But what can I do?" She shrugged. "I'll be thinking of you."

"In Paris," he said, rolling his eyes.

"You can beat Lincoln without me, Scotty."

"No. You're my good-luck charm," he said, only half kidding.

"That's what I am?" she cried, pretending to be offended. "I'm a good-luck charm? That's why you keep me around?"

He nodded, teasing her. He liked it when her green eyes lit up, and her face got all fiery. "That's all," he said. Then he quickly turned serious again. "You're missing the dance and everything."

"Oh, come on, Scotty," she cried, giving him a hard, playful shove. "You don't care about the Homecoming dance, do you? You *really* wanted to stand up in front of all those gawking creeps — I mean, all of our classmates — and be crowned Homecoming King and Queen?"

He turned his glance toward the house. The band was taking a break, but people stayed on the terrace, standing in small groups, talking and laughing.

"I know it's all bogus," he began.

"Yes. It's totally ridiculous," she interrupted.

"But it's kind of an honor," he continued seriously. "And it *is* our last Homecoming dance. I mean, we'll be graduating and everything. I mean . . ." His voice drifted off. He felt embarrassed. Everything he was saying sounded so nerdy.

She looked up at him, holding onto his arm, leaning against him, but didn't say anything.

"Well, you know how everyone expects us to be the perfect couple," he said. "I'll have to answer a million questions. 'Where's Lora?' 'Why aren't you going to the dance?' 'Did you and Lora have a fight?' " He shook his head. "It's going to be totally bogus."

"Hey, I just had a funny idea," Lora said, a sly grin forming on her face, her emerald eyes catching the light from the half moon in the clear sky above them.

"Huh?"

"I think it would be really funny if you got a date to the dance."

He stared at her, his face filled with confusion. "What? What do you mean?"

She chuckled. "You know. Ask somebody else to the dance. It would be great. You'd show up with some other girl, and everyone would totally freak!"

He studied her face, trying to decide if she was serious or not. "You're kidding — right?"

"Of *course* I'm kidding," she replied. "But it *would* freak everyone out, wouldn't it?"

"You have a weird brain," he said. He wrapped his arms around her waist and kissed her.

The party ended a little after midnight. Scotty's mother had taken Denny home a few hours earlier. Now, suddenly feeling very tired, Scotty said good night and thanked Mr. and Mrs. DeMarco.

Lora, yawning loudly, walked him to the front door. "Don't look so sad," she said. "I'll only be gone a week. I'll send you a postcard from the Eiffel Tower. And I'll think of you all the time. I promise." She gave him a long, sweet kiss.

"See you in a week," he said glumly. He started out the door.

"Be good," she called after him. "Stay out of trouble."

Trouble? Scotty thought, heading to his car. What a strange thing to say.

How could *I* ever get into trouble?

# Chapter 3

Scotty stormed into the locker room and heaved his helmet across the room. It hit a locker with a loud *clang* and bounced onto the floor.

"Come on, man," Bender urged, slapping Scotty's shoulder pad. "We'll get 'em next half. It's not so bad."

"It's nine to nothing," Scotty growled, kicking his helmet hard as it rolled up to him on the cement floor.

"Hey, we'll catch 'em," Barker, a running back, yelled, sitting down on the bench across from Scotty. "I almost broke one, you know. If I hadn't slipped . . ."

Scotty looked toward the doorway as his teammates entered, most of them downcast and silent.

I'm letting them down, he thought, picking up his helmet, inspecting the scratch he had made by heaving it into the locker.

I'm letting them down.

"We've been down before," Bender said, untying

his cleats so he could tie them again. "It's no big deal."

"I know I'm going to break one," Barker said, after guzzling about a quart of Gatorade. "Just give me the ball over right tackle. Their whole right side is slow, man. I can get around 'em."

"I should have gotten rid of the ball," Scotty said quietly to Bender. "I never should've let 'em get me in the end zone."

"It was my fault," Bender said. "I let that guy through. He just rolled over me like a tank. He must weigh three hundred pounds. And he's only a sophomore."

Scotty grabbed a paper cup of Gatorade and downed it. Then he took a towel and wiped the perspiration off his face. From out in the stadium, he could hear the band going through its Homecoming routine. What was that song they were playing? "Zip-a-Dee-Doo-Dah"?

"I just lost my concentration," he said glumly, scratching his head. "I should've grounded the ball, just heaved it or something. Instead I stood there like a jerk and ate it."

He reached into his locker and pulled out his black-and-silver Raiders cap.

I'm letting them all down, he thought. On Homecoming.

At least, Lora isn't here to watch me blow it.

Maybe that's the problem, he thought. Lora isn't here to watch. At the party last weekend, he was only kidding about her being his good-luck charm.

But it was obvious he performed better when he knew she was there, watching him, cheering him on.

Up at the front, across from the showers, Coach Hawkins slammed a locker with his fist, his usual way of getting their attention when they were losing at halftime. "You can beat these guys," he said, his high-pitched voice echoing off the low ceiling. "You just have to execute. It all comes down to who executes best."

"You wear that Raiders cap in the shower?" Bender asked, grabbing it off Scotty's head and examining it.

Scotty grabbed it back. "It's sort of a good-luck cap. Lora gave it to me."

Maybe that's your problem," Bender said, finishing with his cleats, leaning forward to grin right in Scotty's face. "You're thinking about the dance."

"I'm not going to the dance," Scotty said, his eyes on the coach, who was diagramming a complicated defensive formation on the small chalkboard.

"Huh? Say what?"

"You heard me," Scotty said edgily. "Lora is in Paris, remember?"

"I don't believe it!" Bender exclaimed, grabbing a plastic water bottle, tilting it over his head, and letting a stream of water run down his face. "The quarterback and the head cheerleader won't be at Homecoming?"

"You can go in my place," Scotty said dryly. He tapped his hands nervously against the bench. He hated halftime. It was always his most nervous time of the game. "You got a date, Bender?"

"Yeah," Bender nodded, drying his face with a towel.

"With who?"

"I don't remember. I called so many girls. I don't remember which one said yes." He laughed.

Scotty forced a laugh, but he was thinking about the game. And about Lora.

My good-luck charm, he thought.

"Hey — did you hear me?" Coach Hawkins cried, glaring at Scotty.

Scotty looked up, startled. "Yeah, I heard you," he lied.

"Well, let's see you do it," Hawkins squeaked. "You guys can beat Lincoln in your sleep."

"We just can't beat 'em when we're awake!" Bender whispered.

"Let's get out there," Hawkins yelled, heading for the door. "Win one for the Gipper!"

He said it every week. No one really knew why.

"Go Tigers!" someone yelled.

"Go Tigers!" several voices repeated.

I've got to get up for this, Scotty thought. I'm not going to be a loser on Homecoming. No way!

He jumped to his feet and stood up on the bench so the rest of the team could see him. "Let's kick their butts!" he shouted, gesturing with his helmet high over his head. "Let's kick their butts! Go Tigers!"

His cheers got them all shouting enthusiastically.

That's more like it, he thought.

Pulling on his helmet, he jogged out of the locker room, and led his team onto the field. His heart began to pound as he stepped under the bright, white lights, the cheers from the bleachers rising over the drums of the departing marching band.

He ran down the line of players, slapping everyone a high five, a tradition he had started. The quarterback has to be a leader, he told himself.

Now I'm going to show them I'm a leader.

Whoops of victory pierced the silence of the locker room as the Tigers swept in after the game, laughing, cheering, shoving each other, butting heads, a noisy, sweaty celebration that Coach Hawkins couldn't stop if he wanted to.

"We shut 'em out! We shut 'em out!" Bender was screaming, swatting his towel wildly at anyone who passed.

Well, we *did* shut them out in the second half, Scotty thought, joining the celebration, chanting along with his teammates. The final score was 14–9. But, secretly, Scotty felt disappointed. The defense had been responsible for both Tiger touchdowns, scoring the last one on a fumble recovery in the final two minutes.

Of course, the stadium erupted into total bedlam. And Scotty was thrilled that they were going to win. But happy as he was, Scotty wished that he had had a little more to do with the Tigers' victory.

Actually, he had played his worst game of the season. He had only completed four or five passes in the second half, all of them for short yardage. He hadn't been able to move the team well at all. And after he messed up a handoff in the beginning of the fourth quarter, Coach Hawkins had actually taken him out for one series of downs, something he hadn't done all season.

I'm glad Lora wasn't here to see this game, he thought, as he joined the raucous cheers, slapped hands, laughed and shouted with his teammates, and pretended he was as happy as they were.

The only way Coach Hawkins was able to stop the locker-room victory party was by blowing his whistle until his round face grew red as a balloon, and then reminding them that they all had to appear at the traditional Homecoming bonfire behind the stadium in less than ten minutes.

After a quick shower, Scotty got into his street clothes, pulled on his down jacket and his Raiders cap, and started to the door, intending to hurry home and skip the bonfire.

"Hey — Singleton!"

It was Bender, pulling a green-and-white Glenview sweatshirt over a T-shirt as he chased after Scotty. "Wait up. I'll walk to the bonfire with you."

"Is that what you're wearing to the dance?" Scotty teased. "Couldn't you have at least found a *clean* sweatshirt?"

"Hey, it's almost clean." Bender grinned. And

then he added, "At least, I'm *going* to the dance."

"You really are bogus, man," Scotty said, shaking his head. "You really know how to kick a guy when he's down."

"How can you be down?" Bender asked, pushing open the door. A rush of cold air greeted them, feeling even colder because they had just stepped out of a steamy shower. "We won the game, right? Even though you stunk up the joint." Bender laughed to show he was teasing.

"Hey, watch it," Scotty said edgily.

"Friends have got to be honest with one another, right?" Bender asked.

"Wrong," Scotty said.

"Oh. Then I take it back. You were awesome tonight," Bender said, grinning.

Scotty punched him hard on the shoulder. Then the two of them began to jog around the parking lot to the back of the stadium.

"Hey, we're just in time," Bender said.

Mr. Velasquez, the principal, was holding a long, flaming torch, about to light the bonfire. A crowd of two or three hundred Glenview students, parents, and people from the neighborhood huddled in sweaters, down jackets, and winter coats, looking exaggeratedly bright and colorful under the high stadium lights.

Scotty followed Bender up to the front. Pieces of lumber, old two-by-fours, fireplace logs, sticks, rags, old cushions, newspapers, and assorted flammable items had been piled into a mountain nearly two stories tall.

Across the way, Scotty saw three Glenview policemen eyeing the proceedings warily, shifting nervously, their eyes on Mr. Velasquez's torch. The Homecoming bonfire wasn't the police department's favorite event, Scotty knew. One year, Scotty's freshman year, the celebration had gotten out of hand, and a house had been set aflame.

"Cut the lights!" Velasquez yelled. A few seconds later, the high stadium lights obediently faded out, surrounding everyone in darkness except for the orange-yellow light of the wavering torch.

A strong gust of wind blew past, bending the torch flame, pushing it downward. The crowd grew silent, drew closer. Scotty pulled down his Raiders cap, then shoved his hands into his jeans pockets.

Light the fire already, he thought. It's getting cold out here!

Velasquez, with his usual dramatic flare, raised the torch high over his head, then lowered the flame to the pile of wood. The flames took hold slowly at first. Sticks crackled. A small yellow flame began to spread.

Before long, the entire mountain burst into flame, the orange-yellow light licking up toward the black, starless sky. It's really awesome, Scotty thought, looking around the circle of cheering faces. Everyone looks so orange and warm.

He took a deep breath. It smelled so good. A

branch crackled and broke, making a group of kids jump back. The flames leaped higher and higher. The fire had become a pulsating, yellow mountain, warm and alive.

"Who brought the marshmallows?" someone shouted.

It got a pretty big laugh.

"Look out — here comes Smokey the Bear!" someone else shouted.

This remark got only groans.

Scotty stepped a little closer, allowing the darting, bright flames to warm him. Velasquez tossed the torch into the fire, then raised his hands over his head, trying to get everyone's attention.

"We had a victory here tonight!" Velasquez shouted in his booming, deep voice. "Let's let the team know we appreciate them. Let's really hear it for the Fighting Tigers!"

This was the excuse the crowd was waiting for to go wild. A deafening cheer rose up, kids slapped hands, and hats and gloves were tossed into the fire. A shoving match started between a group of guys very near the fire, and the three policemen moved quickly to break it up.

The crowd started to chant, "Tigers! Tigers! Tigers!" And when the team paraded in a single line in front of the fire, the wild cheers and celebrating started all over again. Scotty got the biggest cheer of all. He grinned and waved at everyone, holding his hands over his head in a double victory sign.

What a night! Scotty thought happily. He wished

Lora were there. It would've been so much more fun with her.

And then suddenly the crowd was quieting down again, and Velasquez, his face bright red in the glowing firelight, was starting to talk. "We have another bonfire tradition," he shouted.

Scotty searched the crowd for Bender, but couldn't find him. Faces looked strange and distorted in the orange light. A picture of rows and rows of jack-o'-lanterns popped into his mind.

What was Velasquez going on about?

". . . when we crown the Homecoming King and Queen," the principal's voice boomed over the crackling and spitting of the fire.

What? Scotty wondered. What is he saying?

"And so I'd like to call our Homecoming King and Queen up here right now!" Velasquez shouted enthusiastically. "Scotty and Lora — get up here where everyone can see you!"

"Oh, no," Scotty groaned out loud. "Didn't anyone tell him?" He could feel his heart sink down to his feet.

"Scotty and Lora! Let's give it up for them!" Velasquez shouted.

Didn't anyone tell him Lora isn't here? Scotty thought. What am I going to do? This is so embarrassing.

As the crowd cheered, he realized he had no choice. Slowly, hands shoved in his pockets, keeping his eyes on the ground, he made his way toward Velasquez.

Oh, please, let me die right here, he thought. Before the jokes start. Before everyone has a good time laughing at me.

"Lora? Where are you?" Velasquez called when the cheers died down.

"She stood him up!" some guy screamed.

The crowd roared with laughter.

Scotty felt his face grow hot.

"She had another date!" another joker added.

Another roar of laughter. At Scotty's expense.

"Where's Lora?" Velasquez asked Scotty.

"She's in the parking lot with Bender!" someone shouted.

The crowd thought this was hilarious.

Scotty glared angrily into the fire. He had never been so embarrassed in his life, but he didn't want to let these clowns know they were getting to him.

"Lora isn't here," he told Velasquez, leaning close so the principal could hear him over the crowd. "She's away with her family."

"Oh. Right," Velasquez said, slapping his forehead. "Someone told me that this afternoon." He turned away from Scotty to address the crowd. "Lora is away with her parents. What a shame! But at least we can crown the Homecoming King!"

Scotty gritted his teeth and let himself be crowned with the stupid crown. He felt like a total dweeb.

Finally, after a few cheers by the cheerleaders, the bonfire ceremony was over. People started to wander off in groups, still laughing and cheering.

Scotty tore off the crown and tossed it into the fire. Then, ignoring calls from a couple of friends, he put his head down and started to run at full speed toward the student parking lot. His face still felt hot from the fire. The rush of air was cold and refreshing.

"Singleton — you going to the dance?" someone called.

"Hey — where's Lora?" someone else yelled.

He ignored them and kept running. A car squealed out of the parking lot, burning rubber as it roared off down Fairwood Street. "Good game, Scotty!" a guy yelled from a car as Scotty ran past. He acknowledged the compliment with a quick wave, but kept running.

His car, the old Pontiac his mom had bought secondhand, came into view at the very end of the lot. Scotty slowed to a walk and reached into his jacket pocket for the car keys.

He was struggling to unlock the front door when he saw something down low against the fence.

It was a girl.

What was she doing down there? Was she okay?

Scotty stepped back from his car and walked over to her. As he came closer, he saw that she was on her knees, leaning over a bicycle, which was lying on its side.

She was wearing a thin, pale green windbreaker. Her back was turned to him. In the white light suspended over the parking lot, he could see that she had long, red hair, which flowed down to her waist.

Hearing him approach, she turned her head and gave him a shy smile. "Hi," she said breathily.

# Chapter 4

"Flat tire?" Scotty asked.

"Yeah." She made a face.

"That's really bogus," he said, shaking his head.

She's very pretty, he thought. Her long, red hair falling loose behind her was really wild and sexy. And she had a high forehead, and big, brown eyes, and full, red lips.

He thought she looked very dramatic. Like an actress.

I've seen her around school, he thought. But he couldn't remember her name.

"It's a pretty cold night for a bike," he said.

"You want to buy me a car?" she cracked. Then she laughed to soften the remark. She had a light, breathy laugh, like her voice.

She climbed to her feet. He was surprised by how short she was. Her head didn't come up to his shoulders. She looked frail and light in the thin windbreaker, which flapped in the wind. "I think it's a puncture," she said, and kicked at the tire. "I'll have to walk it home."

"How about a lift?" Scotty said, pointing to his car. "We can toss the bike in my trunk."

She looked so light and fragile, as if a strong wind might blow her away.

"Thanks," she said, her big, brown eyes examining him. "I'm Shannon Smith."

Right, he thought. Shannon Smith. He remembered her now. She had only been at Glenview a year or so. He'd seen her sitting in the lunchroom by herself. She didn't seem to have many friends. He remembered her wild red hair.

"I'm Scotty Singleton," he said.

"I know." She looked down at her bike. "Everyone knows *you*," she added, her voice a whisper.

He raked his hand back through his short hair. He suddenly felt awkward, nervous. "So? Want a lift?"

Another car squealed out of the parking lot, the kids inside yelling and singing, the radio blaring. He looked around. The lot was empty now, except for him and Shannon.

"Thanks," she said. "I'm pretty cold." She bent over to pick up the bike. He helped her carry it over to his trunk. Then he popped the trunk and shoved it in.

She lowered her dark eyes, smiled at him, a teasing smile, and slid into the passenger seat. He climbed in behind the wheel and started the engine.

"Aren't you going to the dance?" she asked, toying with a strand of her hair, tangling it and untangling it around her fingers.

"No," Scotty said uncomfortably. He rubbed his cold hands together, waiting for the car to warm up.

"I don't have a date, either," she said softly, playing with her hair. She reached over and touched the back of his hand. "Thanks for rescuing me." Her hand was surprisingly warm. He could still feel the warmth of it after she pulled it away.

He backed up, then headed out of the narrow lot. Up at the school, he could see couples heading in to the dance. He looked for Bender, curious to see who Bender's date was, but didn't see him.

I'm sure I'll hear all about it tomorrow, he thought.

He glanced over at Shannon as he pulled into the street. He liked the way she nibbled at her bottom lip. She glanced back at him, shyly.

"You were good tonight," she said softly.

"You mean at the game?" IIe shook his head. "I was bogus. Totally bogus."

"No, you weren't," she protested, letting go of her hair, dropping her hand to her lap. She scratched the knee of her jeans with slender fingers. "We won, didn't we?"

"No thanks to me," he said moodily, turning onto Park Street.

"Are you always real modest?" she asked, touching the back of his hand again.

Her touch sent a shock of electricity up his arm. "Where do you live?" he asked.

"At Sharpes Corners," she said, looking out the

window. "You know, in the Old Village."

"Yeah, sure," he said. He didn't go to the Old Village much. None of his friends lived there. The houses were old and small and close together. He remembered hearing on TV about a big effort to restore the Old Village to its former glory, or something.

"Do you like football?" he asked, glancing away from the road to look at her. She was playing with her hair again, winding it around one hand. He realized he was very attracted to her.

"Not much," she replied and then laughed at her answer. "But I like going to the games. My brothers all like football. I guess that's why I don't like it."

"How many brothers do you have?" he asked, slowing for the light at Harbor Crossing.

"Three," she said, making a face. "Three big louts."

"Let me guess," he said. "You don't like your brothers?"

"We don't have much in common," she said, sliding down in the seat, raising her knees to the dashboard. "They're all older than me. They're all big. Really big. The oldest one, Kurt, was a pro wrestler. A pro. Do you believe it?"

"Wow," Scotty said. "Remind me to stay on your good side!"

He had meant it as a joke, but he saw her face turn serious. "I will," she said softly.

They drove in silence for a while. She's so pretty,

Scotty thought. Why doesn't she have a date tonight?

"You want to stop and get a hamburger or something?" he asked. The words popped out. He hadn't really thought about it. As he said it, it felt as if someone else were talking.

I haven't been out with another girl in . . . *how many* years? he asked himself.

Never, he realized.

He'd been with Lora since sixth grade.

Well, I'm not really *out* with Shannon, he told himself. This isn't a date or anything. I'm just helping her get home. So what's wrong with stopping for a hamburger on the way?

"I'd love to," she said breathily, her voice so soft he could barely hear her.

"Great," he said. "I'm always starving after a game." He turned the car around and started to drive to Henry's, the hamburger restaurant near school where everyone hung out. He had gone a couple of blocks when he decided that wasn't a good idea.

There'll probably be a lot of kids I know there, he thought. And they'll see me with Shannon. And they'll start making jokes. Or they'll start making up stories about me. Or word will get back to Lora that I had a date with another girl.

Why look for trouble?

"Know any good places in the Old Village?" he asked.

She nibbled at her bottom lip, her expression thoughtful. "Well, there's a Burger Basket on Ridge just before the railroad tracks."

"Sounds perfect," he said. "Let's go there."

"Okay," she said softly.

Did she sound a little disappointed, or was he just imagining it?

A few minutes later, he found the Burger Basket and pulled into the lot. There were only two other cars in the lot, he noticed with relief.

This looks like a pretty rough neighborhood, he thought, looking around at the low, dark buildings and empty lots across from the hamburger restaurant.

As they walked in through the glass doors, Shannon took his hand. Her hand felt so warm, so light, so fragile. She smiled up at him, a playful smile. Her hair smelled sweet, like cinammon and oranges.

He guided her to a booth in back, away from the windows.

Hey, I'm not doing anything wrong, Scotty thought.

So why do I feel so strange?

# Chapter 5

He liked the way she kept touching his hand as she talked. She was always gesturing with her small hands, tugging at her hair, reaching across the table to touch his arm or his hand, as if she had known **him** for years.

And he liked the way her red hair fell, tangled and wild. Lora was always fussing with her hair. It had to be perfect, not a hair out of place. But Shannon didn't seem to care. She tossed her hair back over her shoulder as she talked, or twirled a strand around her fingers, or tugged at it, smiling, as she leaned forward to listen to him.

She smiled at him with those dark, pouty lips. Her smile was knowing, almost smug, not at all an innocent little girl's smile.

The restaurant was empty except for a pair of silent old men hunched over cups of coffee, and four tough-looking teenagers Scotty had never seen before in a booth next to the window.

He felt comfortable knowing that no one from

school would see him here. And he felt excited sitting here with Shannon, a kind of excitement he had never felt in his life. The excitement of doing something wrong.

Or of *thinking* about doing something wrong.

Of course, he kept reassuring himself, there's nothing wrong with having a hamburger with someone and driving her home. It's not like Lora and I are *married*, he thought, scolding himself for feeling guilty.

"You're a senior, right?" Shannon asked, wiping hamburger juice off her chin with a paper napkin.

"Yeah. You, too?"

She nodded. "What are you doing after graduation?"

"Oh, I'm going to Princeton," he said casually. "Where are you going?"

She looked down. "Probably look for a job, I guess."

He could feel his face redden. She must really think I'm a rich jerk, he thought. Why did I assume she was going to college?

"I'm . . . uh . . . hoping to get a scholarship," he added quickly. "My mom can't really afford it unless I get a scholarship."

"Where's your dad?" she asked.

Scotty was a little startled by the question. He responded with a broad shrug, as if to say, "Who knows?"

For some reason, this struck Shannon as funny.

Her laugh was high and fragile, like the tinkling of a glass wind chime.

They talked for an hour after their hamburgers were finished. Scotty was usually exhausted after a football game, but being with her was keeping him wide awake.

They didn't have much in common. She hated school, hated Glenview, seemed generally unhappy with her life but didn't have any plan for changing it. Unlike Scotty and Lora and their friends, she didn't seem to have any ambition, any goals, any dream.

When he asked her what she'd really like to do with her life, she had to think about it. Finally, tugging at her hair, she said, "I don't know. Be a rock star maybe. Maybe be like Madonna."

As he drove her home, she slid low in the seat, her knees on the dashboard. She turned on the radio and cranked up the volume until the entire car throbbed and vibrated, and sang along in her whispery voice, ignoring Scotty entirely except to point the directions to her house.

The house was a little box, so small Scotty nearly drove right past it. It was entirely dark. He drove up the dirt driveway, his headlights rolling over a rusted pickup truck, tireless, up on cinder blocks in the middle of the narrow front yard. The house was white clapboard but looked as if it hadn't been painted for a long time.

Scotty clicked off the blaring radio.

"Home sweet home," Shannon said, sighing.

How do her three big wrestler brothers fit into that tiny house? Scotty wondered.

He jumped out, ran around the car through the twin white headlight beams, and pulled open the car door. She reached up her hands, and he pulled her to her feet on the soft dirt drive.

To his surprise, she didn't let go of his hands. Squeezing them tightly in her warm hands, she leaned forward, raised herself on tiptoe, and pressed her mouth against his.

Her lips were wet and burning hot.

Her soft hair brushed against his face.

She leaned forward, pressing against him. He started to back away, but realized she didn't want the kiss to end. Giving in to it, he put his arms around her.

She kissed harder, harder.

Hungrily.

Finally she let go. Backed away. Smiled up at him. That sexy, knowing smile.

Wow, he thought.

"Thanks for the lift," she said, breathing hard.

"Uh . . . no problem." He couldn't think of anything else to say. "Hey — almost forgot your bike."

He could still feel the heat of her mouth on his, could still feel the brush of her hair against his face. Feeling crazy and exhausted and excited and confused all at once, he walked quickly to the trunk, opened it, and pulled out the bike.

"You can just leave it here. One of my brothers

will fix it for me in the morning," she said, pulling the light plastic windbreaker around her.

He set it down beside the drive.

"Shannon — are you busy tomorrow night?"

"What?"

He walked back toward her. "Do you want to go to a movie or something?"

She smiled. The half moon in the dark, starless sky above them sparkled in her eyes.

I don't believe I just asked her out, he thought. What am I *doing*?

"Yes. Okay. Neat," she said.

"I'll come by about seven."

What am I *doing*?

She turned and ran quickly to the dark house without looking back. He climbed into the car, closed the door, and looked for her. But she had disappeared. Probably already inside.

The car bumped over the dirt driveway as he backed out to the street.

One date is no big deal, Scotty thought.

Lora is off in Paris and London having the time of her life. Why shouldn't I have a little fun, too?

Besides, Lora will never know. . . .

# Chapter 6

Saturday was gray but not as blustery. It felt to Scotty more like a day in late September than November. He had slept in, then had a long, leisurely breakfast. When Bender came over to help rake leaves as they had arranged, Scotty was still in his pajamas.

"You sick or something?" Bender asked, walking in through the back door without knocking, as usual.

He startled Scotty from his thoughts about Shannon.

"You sure look serious this morning," Bender said, grabbing a piece of cold bacon off Scotty's plate and stuffing it into his mouth.

"Oh. I was just thinking about . . . the game," Scotty said, thinking quickly.

"Great game," Bender said, wandering around the kitchen on his long, lanky legs, looking for more food to scavenge.

"Yeah," Scotty agreed, trying to clear the fog from his head. "I'll get dressed. Be right back, man."

"Sure. I'll just make myself a sandwich or something," Bender called after him.

He eats as much as a herd of elephants, Scotty thought in his room, pulling on jeans and a sweatshirt. But he's the skinniest, lightest tackle on the team.

A few minutes later, they were raking the front yard, attacking the large, dead leaves with enthusiasm. "Hey, you guys," Mrs. Singleton called, poking her head out of an upstairs window. "What are you doing?" She had a pink bath towel wrapped around her head.

"What are we doing?" Scotty shouted up to her. "What does it *look* like we're doing? We're raking the leaves!"

"Well, why are you raking in one direction and Bender raking in the other?" she demanded. "You're making two separate piles!"

Scotty and Bender looked at each other. "That's just the way we rake," Scotty replied.

"The earth is round, Mrs. Singleton," Bender added. "Scotty and I are bound to meet sometime!"

"Very funny!" she called sarcastically, and slammed the window shut.

"No sense of humor," Bender muttered, leaning on the rake, then pretending to fall off it. He toppled sideways to the ground. Bender loved falling down. He thought it was hilarious. And he was very good at it.

"How was the dance?" Scotty asked, thinking about Shannon as he started to rake again.

I can't believe I asked her out, he thought. Am I really going to go through with it?

Of course.

He realized he hadn't heard Bender's reply.

"Hey, everyone was asking about you and Lora," Bender said. He was raking with the wrong side of the rake. Anything for a laugh.

"Stop goofing. We'll never get finished," Scotty said, laughing.

"So what did *you* do after the game?" Bender asked.

"Oh, I just went home and . . . watched a video," Scotty told him, avoiding his glance.

"Yeah? What'd you see?"

"Uh . . . I don't remember, man. It was just some dumb movie Denny rented."

I'm such a bad liar, Scotty thought. I can never think fast enough when I want to tell a lie, and I'll bet my face is bright red.

Bender, raking in long, slow sweeps, didn't seem to notice. "So what are you doing tonight? Want to come over and shoot some pool or something?"

"I can't," Scotty said quickly. Too quickly.

Bender looked over at him. "How come? Hot date?"

"Yeah, sure," Scotty said sarcastically, still avoiding Bender's eyes.

Bender laughed at the idea. "Lora would murder you," he said.

"I . . . uh . . . have to study tonight," Scotty lied.

One lie after another, he thought, feeling guilty.

"You? Study?" Bender exclaimed, and fell backwards into the leaf pile he had made. "I thought you got your perfect grades without cracking a book." He sat up. Flat, brown leaves clung to his hair. "Besides, man, they already took you at Princeton. Why knock yourself out?"

"I can't just veg out all the rest of this year," Scotty replied. "Then people would think I was *you*!" He laughed at his own joke and tossed the rake to the ground. "This is boring," he said, helping Bender to his feet. "Let's go check out Ernie."

"You still have that snake?" Bender asked, loping along behind Scotty, around the side of the house to the backyard.

"Yeah. I built this neat cage for him," Scotty said. "On the side of the garage. I put a heater in it and everything, and Ernie gets plenty of sun and fresh air. Mom wouldn't let me keep him in the house since he got so big. She's scared of him."

"Scared of snakes? How weird!" Bender exclaimed.

Scotty gave him a playful shove. Bender pretended to go flying into the side of the garage.

They stopped in front of the large mesh-and-glass cage Scotty had built. "Hey, you've practically got a whole tree in there," Bender said, peering in from the top.

"Well, Ernie's a tree snake," Scotty explained. "I wanted him to feel at home."

The bright green snake was coiled up in the V formed by two branches, its head hidden from view.

"That's the most amazing color," Bender said. "That green is almost neon. I'd like to have a shirt that color."

"I thought *all* your shirts were that color," Scotty joked.

"Just the dress-up ones," Bender said. "So, how about it, Scottso — change your mind. Come over tonight. You can study next year."

"No, really, I can't," Scotty insisted. "I've . . . just got a lot of work to do."

Going out with Shannon has *got* to be wrong, he thought. And here I am, lying to my best buddy.

But so what?

So I'll be *bad* for just one night.

"Hey, Scotty!" His mother yelled from the back door. "Scotty — you back there?"

He stepped away from the cage. "Yeah, Mom!"

"Mail just came," she shouted. "Come look. You got a postcard from Lora!"

Scotty pulled his Raiders cap low over his forehead as he and Shannon walked out of the movie theater. "How'd you like it?" he asked, his hand on her back, guiding her toward the car.

He had taken her to the old Westside theater in the next town, deliberately staying as far away as possible from the tenplex at the mall, or anywhere else he might be recognized.

"It was pretty cute," she said thoughtfully. "But I didn't get some of the humor, I don't think. It was very dry."

He had watched her during the movie and hadn't been able to tell if she was enjoying it at all. For the most part, she sat through it, expressionless, nibbling on her lower lip. Near the end of the movie, she had taken his hand between hers and held it tightly, staring straight ahead at the screen.

He couldn't help stealing glances at her. She was wearing a tight wool sweater and a very short green leather skirt over sheer tights.

I can't believe I'm sitting here with her, he thought.

He was so nervous and excited, he could barely follow the movie.

"I thought John Candy was a riot," he said, trying to keep the conversation going. So far, it hadn't been as easy to talk to her as the night before.

"John Candy. Is he the fat one?" she asked, lowering herself into the car.

Of *course* he's the fat one, Scotty thought as he walked around the car and slid into the driver's seat. Who *else* would he be?

He was starting to think that asking Shannon out was a big mistake when, without warning, she leaned across the gearshift and kissed him.

She smelled so sweet, like oranges. Her hair brushed lightly against his face, tickling his cheeks, sending a chill down his neck.

She leaned back into her seat, smiling at him, licking her lips.

He took a deep breath. "Would you like to go up to Rainer Point?" he asked softly, suddenly feeling nervous. Everyone knew that Rainer Point was a big make-out spot. How would Shannon react to that idea?

Shannon laughed and shook her head no.

Scotty felt embarrassed. Too fast, he thought. I moved too fast. That wasn't too cool of me. I'm such a jerk! And now she thinks I'm a jerk, too!

But then she touched the back of his hand and said, "Let's go to my house instead."

He looked over to see a very playful smile on her face. "What?"

"Let's go to my house," she whispered. "We'll be all alone. My brothers are away, and my parents are at an all-night party."

"Really?" he gulped, his voice cracking.

She nodded her head, her long hair covering her face. "Really," she said, pulling the tangles of red hair away.

He turned the car around and headed toward her house. The night was clear and cold. There were a lot of cars on the road, people out looking for fun on Saturday night. An accident at Penn Crossing had the traffic at a standstill.

They sat in awkward silence. She smiled at him. He tried to think of something to talk about. But they'd already gone over last night's football game again, and they'd already discussed the movie, and school, and the weather.

He was grateful when Shannon reached over and turned on the radio. Again, she turned it up until the car felt about to explode, and sang along, so softly he could see her lips moving but couldn't hear her sing.

We don't have much in common, he realized. This will have to be our only date.

But she really is a babe!

When he reached her house on Sharpes Corners, he pulled up the dirt drive and cut the headlights and the engine. The house was completely dark, as the night before.

As soon as they got inside, she slammed the front door. Then, staring boldly, almost challengingly into his eyes, she pulled off his Raiders cap and tossed it across the dark room.

Then she started covering his face with kisses.

Wow! he thought. This is *awesome!*

"You're *my* baby now," she whispered, holding his head with both hands as she kissed him.

"You're *my* baby now."

# Chapter 7

Scotty was awakened the next morning by the phone ringing. He stirred, shook his head as if trying to shake away his sleepiness, and pulled himself up to a sitting position.

Downstairs, he could hear the thunder of Denny's sneakers against the living room floor as he ran to answer the phone. "I'll get it!" Denny screamed.

Scotty yawned and stretched. His head felt like a lead weight. When had he finally rolled back home? It must have been after one in the morning.

And what time was it now? He tried to focus on the digital clock beside his bed, but it was a blur.

"Scotty — phone for you!" Denny shouted from the foot of the stairs, loud enough to wake the dead. "It's a girl!"

"Huh?" Scotty said aloud, scratching his head. Could it be Lora?

No. Her plane doesn't arrive until this evening.

He lumbered over to his desk, tossed a dirty T-shirt out of the way, and picked up the phone. "Hello?" His voice sounded low and husky.

The voice on the other end woke him up immediately.

"Good morning, baby," Shannon chirped.

"Huh? Shannon?" His throat felt dry. He realized his heart was pounding.

"I had such a good time last night," she said softly.

"What time is it?" Scotty asked.

Why is she calling me? he wondered. What does she want?

"It's early, but I just wanted to talk to you," Shannon replied in a little girl's voice. "Did you dream about me?"

"Listen, Shannon — " he started. He could hear his mom padding down the hall, coming toward his room.

"Are you coming over to see me today, baby?" Shannon asked in a tiny voice.

"No, listen. Shannon, I — "

Mrs. Singleton poked her head into the room. Her platinum hair was piled high on her head, tied with a purple ribbon, but she was still in her bathrobe. "Who is it, dear?" she asked, her expression disapproving.

"I'll have to call you later about that," Scotty said quickly into the phone. "Talk to you later, okay?" He hung up the receiver. "Just a girl from school," he told his mother, trying to sound nonchalant. "She had a question about the psych homework."

"So early?" Mrs. Singleton asked, turning her disapproving gaze on the bedtable clock.

Scotty could read it now. It was 8:08. Sunday morning.

"I guess she was getting an early start on it," Scotty said. "I probably should, too."

He hated lying. Whenever he did it, he had the feeling lights lit up on his face, blinking on and off, "Lie! Lie! Lie!"

"When did you get in last night, Scotty?" she asked, tightening the belt on the loose-fitting robe.

"Not too late." Another lie.

"Well, I'm just going down to start breakfast. You want pancakes this morning?"

"No. Something light," Scotty said, making a face.

He stood leaning on the desk, listening to her slippers thud down the stairs. He heard her ask Denny what he was doing up so early. Denny already had the TV in the living room going. Scotty could hear the loud boings and crashes of some kind of cartoon show.

I've got to tell Shannon not to call, he decided.

I've got to make it really clear to her that it's over between us. I mean, we just had the one date. It was just a one-time thing.

When he had said good night to her, standing in the dark, narrow hallway of her tiny house, he tried to let her know that he wouldn't be seeing her again.

"I'll call you sometime." That's what he had told her. "I'll call you sometime."

The meaning of that is pretty clear, he told himself.

Shannon had smiled back at him in the dark, but she had to know what he was telling her.

It was over, over, over.

After all, Lora would be home tonight. He realized he couldn't wait to see her. An entire week was a long time without seeing Lora.

Much too long.

He showered and pulled on a pair of gray sweatpants and a matching sweatshirt. Maybe Bender and I can go to the playground and play a little roundball, he thought. Shoot some hoops. Or maybe a long bike ride. He felt like getting some exercise.

He was down in the kitchen, finishing his cornflakes, sitting at the breakfast counter with Denny and his mother, when the phone rang again.

Scotty started toward the wall phone beside the refrigerator, but Denny got there first. "Who is it?" he asked into the receiver. Denny never bothered to say hello. He always picked up the phone and asked, "Who is it?"

He held the phone out to Scotty. "It's for you," he said. Then he grinned. "The same girl!"

Scotty caught the surprised expression on his mother's face as he hurried over and took the phone from his little brother. "Hello?"

"Hi, baby," Shannon said in her whispery voice.

"Whatcha doin'? You didn't call me back."

"Uh . . . listen . . . uh . . ." Scotty looked back at his mother and Denny. They were both staring at him. "I'm going to take this call upstairs, okay?" he said. "It's homework stuff." He handed the receiver to Denny. "Hang up when I get upstairs, okay?"

Grinning, Denny took the receiver and held it up to his ear. "I can hear her breathing," he said.

"Just hold it for a second," Scotty snapped. He hurried out of the kitchen, through the front hall, and up the stairs to his room, thinking hard about how to get Shannon to stop calling him.

"What does she think she's doing?" he muttered to himself aloud.

As he picked up the phone in his room, he was breathing hard from taking the stairs three at a time. "Hi, Shannon. Listen — "

He heard giggling, realized Denny was still on the kitchen phone.

"Denny?"

"Yeah?"

"Get off the phone. Hang up — now."

Silence.

Scotty waited for the click, the signal that Denny had hung up.

"Denny?"

"Yeah?"

*"Get off the phone!"*

Denny giggled, made a rude noise with his lips, then finally hung up.

"Who was that?" Shannon asked.

"My dumb kid brother," Scotty said. "He's really bogus."

"He sounds really cute," she said. "I can't wait to meet him."

Meet him? thought Scotty. Why would she ever meet Denny?

"When are you coming over, baby?" she asked. "I'm kinda lonely."

"I can't come over, Shannon," he said. He decided to be really straight with her.

"What?"

"Listen, I'm, like, really busy. You know, with school and everything. And I've got stuff to do around here for my mom. And a lot of studying to do."

"Didn't you have a good time last night?" she asked, suddenly sounding hurt.

"Of course, I did," he told her. "I had a great time, Shannon. Really. But . . . but you shouldn't call. I'm very busy now." He took a deep breath. "And I'm not going to be able to go out with you again."

She giggled. "Aw, you're teasing me. Right?"

"No, really. I'm not," he said. "I have to go now. Good-bye, okay? I'll see you in school next week."

He hung up before she could reply.

The receiver was all wet from his hand perspiring. He stood there for a moment, leaning on the desk, waiting for his heart to resume its normal pace, staring at the phone, half expecting it to ring again.

But it remained silent.

Feeling a little better, he headed downstairs to finish his breakfast. Denny had returned to the cartoons on TV. His mother was unloading the dishwasher. "I thought I'd go over to Bender's. Maybe play some basketball or something," he told her.

She turned around and stared at him, surprised. "Did you forget?"

"Huh? Forget what?" He picked up a piece of cold toast and chewed it.

"About Denny's school fair? Remember? You promised to help out?"

"What?" Scotty cried. "I did? When did I promise? In my sleep?"

Her expression turned stern. "Come on, Scotty. You promised me. I'm the class mother, remember. How will it look if you don't show?"

"But, Mom — "

"It isn't anything difficult. Just coat-check duty. Come on, Scotty. You promised."

He hated it when his mother whined like that. But it was starting to come back to him. He had been feeling guilty because he'd promised to take Denny out bike riding, but then Lora had come over, and he'd gone off with her instead. And so he'd promised he'd go and help out at Denny's school fair.

"Okay. I'll check coats," he said glumly.

What a boring way to spend a Sunday.

His mother smiled. "Good. It should help the time pass for you. When the fair is over, Lora should be almost home. That's exciting, isn't it?"

"Yeah," he said quietly. He couldn't let on to his mother how pleased he really was that Lora would be back.

"I'm going to play video games at the fair," Denny said, entering the room to get a box of juice from the refrigerator.

"You have video games at home," Scotty said.

"So?" Denny hurried back to his cartoons.

A few hours later, Scotty was in the noisy, crowded front hall of Denny's school, checking coats as parents and kids streamed in for the annual fair. Luckily, it was a clear, dry day, so the coats weren't wet or snow-covered. Across the hall, Mrs. Singleton and two other women were selling tickets from large ticket rolls.

"Where's Lora?" a voice asked.

Scotty, weighed down with two long, down overcoats, turned to see Mrs. Farberson, a friend of his mother's, smiling at him.

"She's in Paris," Scotty said. "With her parents. But she's coming home tonight."

"I don't mean to embarrass you," the large, red-faced woman said, handing Scotty her fur-collared coat, "but you and Lora just make the most wonderful couple."

"Thanks," Scotty said awkwardly.

"I *am* embarrassing you. I'm sorry," Mrs. Farberson said, taking the coat-check ticket from him. "But you're just so cute together."

Scotty smiled, an uncomfortable smile. "Thanks," he said again.

Please go away, he thought.

He hated it when people said that he and Lora were "cute." This wasn't the first time he had heard it. But he wished it were the last.

"I know your mother is so proud of you," she gushed. She turned. "Oh — there's your mother over there. I must go say hello. 'Bye, Scotty. Say hi to Lora for me."

He watched her make her way through the crowd, then went to hang up her coat.

The rest of the afternoon was uneventful. Only three other people asked him where Lora was, two of them, friends of the DeMarcos, commenting on what a wonderful couple they were.

Scotty realized he should have been used to the compliments. He and Lora had been together since sixth grade, after all. But even though he really was nuts about Lora, it never failed to embarrass him when people made a fuss about what a terrific couple they were.

It's *our* business — not theirs, he thought.

That evening, he, Denny, and his mother had just finished dinner, fried chicken and french fries from a take-out place down the street. He was about to go upstairs to do some homework, when the phone rang.

"I'll bet that's Lora," Mrs. Singleton said, glancing at the kitchen clock. "It's early, but I'll bet she's calling you from the airport."

Scotty hurried over to the kitchen wallphone and eagerly grabbed up the receiver. "Hello?"

"Hi, baby. Aren't you coming over tonight?" Shannon half talked, half whispered, more of a plea than a question.

Scotty looked back at his mother, who was staring at him expectantly.

"I'm sorry," he said coldly into the receiver. "We already subscribe to *TV Guide*." He hung up the receiver.

His mother was still staring at him, a thoughtful expression on her face.

"I don't believe those sales people," Scotty complained, shaking his head. "They're so bogus! Can you imagine — calling at dinnertime on Sunday night!"

Why was his mother staring at him like that?

Did she suspect something? Or was he just being paranoid?

He was halfway back to the table when the phone rang again.

# Chapter 8

Scotty hesitated, staring at the phone on the kitchen wall. It rang again.

"Aren't you going to answer it?" his mother asked impatiently.

"Yeah. I guess." He walked over to it, let it ring a third time, then, with a heavy feeling of dread, picked it up. "Hello?"

"Hi, it's me."

It was Lora.

"Lora? Where are you? At home?" he asked feeling happy — and relieved.

"Yes. I'm home. Totally wrecked. The plane was delayed for over an hour."

"How was it?" Mrs. Singleton called from across the room. "Did she have a good time?"

Scotty repeated the question. "I had a *great* time!" Lora exclaimed. "Paris is so beautiful. Like a movie set. Not like a real city at all. I just couldn't believe it, couldn't see enough. One day, yesterday I think, I'm too tired to think clearly, we were at

Montmartre, looking down from way up high, and it started to snow. This gentle, light snow. It was the most beautiful thing I've ever seen. I don't think I'll ever forget that moment."

"Wow!" Scotty said. "Sounds neat!"

"Get down," Lora said.

"What?"

"Oh. Sorry. I was talking to Fluffernutter. *Get down, you dumb cat.* She won't get out of my lap. Scotty, I think Fluffernutter missed me more than you did!"

Scotty forced a laugh. "That's impossible," he said.

"You missed me?" she asked.

"Of course I did," he said. "It was really bogus without you around. It just felt so weird."

He couldn't help it. As he said those words, Shannon forced her way into his mind. He thought of Saturday night in Shannon's steamy, dark living room.

"I'm happy to be back, too. I thought about you all the time," Lora said.

Scotty felt so guilty, his words caught in his throat.

"Scotty — ?"

"Uh . . . listen, Lora, let's spend all of next weekend together, okay? Just having fun. Only the two of us." He heard the clatter of dishes behind him. His mother was clearing the dinner dishes, noisily loading the dishwasher.

"Scotty, have you forgotten? The Junior Chamber of Commerce thing? You know, the Autumn Ball, or whatever they call it?"

"Let's skip it," he urged. He really felt like being with her and no one else. He had to make it up to her for what he had done, for sneaking out with another girl, a girl he had no real interest in.

"We can't skip it, Scotty," Lora said, sighing. "We're being crowned Teens of the Year, remember?"

"So?" he asked, realizing he was sounding just like Denny.

"So? So they're giving us each five hundred dollars," she said.

"Oh. Right. Well," he said, changing his tone, "I'm really looking forward to that!"

She laughed. "Maybe we can sneak out early," she said playfully. "Maybe we'll take the money and run."

"I like the way your mind works," he said.

"Fluffernutter, get down!" she shouted. "Scotty, I'd better get off the phone. I'm so tired. I think I'm still on Paris time. I don't know *what* time it is."

"Okay. See you tomorrow in school," he said, not wanting to hang up.

"Yeah. See you tomorrow," she said softly, and then added, "I missed you."

"Me, too," he said and hung up feeling very guilty.

"Did they have a good time?" Mrs. Singleton

asked, struggling to close the dishwasher. The handle always stuck.

Scotty hurried over to help her. "Yeah. She said it was great. It snowed one day."

"In Paris? That must have been beautiful," she said dreamily. "I've always wanted to see Paris in the snow."

Scotty's mother had never been to Europe. With the two boys to bring up, there was never enough money for such an extravagant trip.

"Well, I'm glad they made it back okay," she said, giving the counter a final wipe with the dish towel.

Scotty suddenly had the urge to get out of the house, to get into the car, to drive somewhere fast, to drive anywhere, to just get away. "I'm going out for a short while," he told his mother, avoiding her glance.

"You going to Lora's?"

"No. She's too tired. I'm just going for a ride, maybe stop at Bender's," he said, heading to the front closet for his jacket.

"On a Sunday night? Don't you have homework?"

"I'll be back in a few minutes," he said impatiently.

"Do what you want." She disappeared up the stairs.

Scotty pulled on his jacket and searched the shelf for his Raiders cap. Rummaging through the scarves and gloves and woolen ski caps, he couldn't find it.

My cap. Where could it be?

And then he realized. He had left it at Shannon's.

Yes. She had tossed it across the room, and he had never retrieved it.

Maybe I should drive over there and get it, he thought, stepping out the door into a blustery, cold night. It *is* my favorite cap, after all.

I'll just knock on the door. Stay on the front stoop. Ask for my cap.

*No way*, he told himself.

No way I'm going back to Shannon's. I'm never going back there. Never.

It was a promise he was making to himself, a solemn promise, to him — and to Lora.

Never.

She can keep the hat.

He climbed into the old Pontiac and drove aimlessly around town for nearly an hour. Houses and shops whirred by in the darkness as a light fog settled in. Scotty paid no attention to where he was or where he was going. He felt like driving, just driving.

He didn't think about anything. The darkness, the cold air, the wisps of soft, gray fog all calmed him. By the time he returned home and pulled the car into the garage, he was feeling very relaxed.

The next morning, he arrived at school early, a little past seven-thirty, and found Shannon waiting for him at his locker.

# Chapter 9

Scotty stopped short, several yards away. "Shannon?" His voice echoed in the empty corridor.

A warm smile spread across her face. She didn't wait for him to come closer. She ran up to him and jumped up to give him a playful kiss on the cheek.

"Surprised?"

"Yeah," he said, taking a step back. He pulled off his backpack and let it slide to the floor.

She was wearing a bright red turtleneck sweater that clashed with her red hair, and tight black denims. Stepping forward quickly, she tilted her head up for another kiss.

"Whoa. Stop," he said sharply.

"It's okay, baby," she replied softly. "It's nice and early. There's no one around."

"Shannon — what are you *doing* here?" Scotty demanded.

"I wanted to see you," she said, tossing her long hair back over one shoulder. "You're my baby now."

"No, I'm not," he said angrily. He picked up the

backpack and slammed it against the wall. "Stop saying that."

Her dark eyes narrowed. "You liked it Saturday night," she said. She looked about to cry.

She's a good actress, he thought.

It made him even angrier.

"Saturday night was great," he told her. "But it was just one date, okay? It was great. But that's it. We can't go out. Okay? We can't."

"But, baby — "

"Shannon — please!" He looked behind him. A few kids were wandering into the building. Lockers were being opened. Voices echoed down the long corridor. "I'm going with someone," he told her. "Someone I'm very serious about. She's very important to me and — "

"Hey, man — how's it going?"

A hand grabbed Scotty's shoulder from behind.

Scotty wheeled around to see Bender grinning down at him. "Where were you yesterday afternoon?" Bender asked. "I called your house and — "

Bender stopped because he noticed Shannon. "Oh," he said, seeing the forlorn expression on Shannon's face and realizing that he had interrupted a conversation. "Sorry, man. I didn't know . . ."

Bender's face filled with embarrassment. Waving his big hand at Scotty, he started to back down the hall.

"No, Bender — wait!" Scotty said. "Wait up!" He picked up his bookbag.

"I've got to get to homeroom," Bender shouted, still looking embarrassed, and disappeared around the corner.

Shannon stepped in front of Scotty, blocking his way. The hall was crowded now. Scotty looked toward the doors, expecting to see Lora come walking in.

"You're not being nice to me, baby," Shannon said, putting a hand gently on the front of Scotty's jacket.

"Shannon, give me a break — "

"I was so nice to you," she said softly, ignoring his anger, not moving her hand from his chest. "But you're not being nice to me." A tear formed in the corner of each eye.

The bell rang.

She lifted her hand off the front of his jacket. The single tears were rolling down her pale cheeks. She turned quickly and ran.

He stared after her, watching her run through the crowded hall, her hair flowing wildly behind her. A few seconds later, she turned the corner and disappeared from view.

Maybe I finally got through to her, he thought. Maybe she finally gets the picture.

Feeling a lot better, he unlocked his locker and got ready to start the school day.


"Shouldn't I get my coat?" Lora asked.

"No. It isn't that cold out. Really," Scotty urged. "You'll see."

She followed him out the door and onto the lawn behind the school. They were both carrying brown paper lunchbags and cartons of milk. It was Scotty's idea to eat their lunch outdoors, not only for the fresh air but for the privacy.

"I feel like you've been gone a lot longer than a week," he said, sitting down under a large maple tree, bare and wintry-looking. He patted the leafy ground beside him. Lora sat down.

"You're just saying that to be sweet," she said, affectionately pressing her forehead against his cheek.

"Yeah, you're right," he said, and laughed, casually putting an arm around her shoulders.

It was so easy being with Lora, he realized. So comfortable. So *right*.

"What have you got?" Lora asked, removing his arm so she could open her lunch.

"Ham and cheese, I think. Every day it's ham and cheese. So boring."

"Well, who packs your lunch?" she asked.

"I do!"

They both laughed.

"It's not too cold out here. You were right," she said, unwrapping her tuna fish sandwich. Half the tuna fish fell out onto her lap.

"Smooth move," Scotty said.

"The food was a little better in Paris," Lora said, picking up a clump of tuna with her hand and popping it into her mouth. "The bread. The bread was the most spectacular thing. I could just live on the bread. It was so good!"

"Better than Wonder Bread?" Scotty joked.

"Hey, Scotty?" Lora's tone suddenly changed.

"Yeah?" he asked, with a mouth full of sandwich.

"Who's that girl?"

"What?"

Lora pointed.

Scotty looked up to see Shannon standing on the walk a few yards away. Her light windbreaker was open, and she had her hands on her hips as she stared intently at Scotty and Lora.

"Why is she looking at us like that?" Lora asked.

"I don't know," Scotty told her. "I've never seen her before."

# Chapter 10

Scotty walked home after school, thinking about Shannon. The sky had turned gray and threatening. Gusting winds tossed waves of dead, brown leaves at his feet, but he stepped through them without noticing.

Shannon, what am I going to do about you? he thought.

How can I get through to you?

It had been so embarrassing at lunch. Shannon had stood there like a statue, staring angrily at Scotty and Lora for the longest time. What did she think I would do? Scotty asked himself. Go running over to her and invite her to join us?

Why can't she take a hint?

I've been straight with her. I've told her exactly how I feel. What more can I do?

He turned the corner onto his block and saw Shannon sitting on his front steps.

Oh, man.

Now what?

She hadn't seen him yet. She was sitting with her head down, her knees tucked between her hands. His first impulse was to turn and run in the other direction.

But that wouldn't do any good, he realized. She'd be sitting there when his mother got home with Denny. And how would he ever explain Shannon to his mother?

No. He had to face her. He had to make her understand that she had to leave him alone.

He took a deep breath and, with long, determined strides, walked over the leaf-strewn lawn to the front stoop. "Hi, Shannon," he said wearily, letting his expression show how unhappy he was to see her.

"You have to break up with her," Shannon said, raising her head slowly. Her eyes were red-rimmed, as if she'd been crying. Her hair was more tangled than usual, one twisted strand falling down over an eye.

"What? Are you crazy?"

She didn't react to him at all, didn't even look at him. "You have to break up with her," she repeated in a low, steady voice.

"Shannon, there's no way I'm breaking up with Lora," Scotty said, standing over her, shifting his weight uncomfortably. He pulled off his backpack and heaved it onto the walk. "No way."

"But you're *my* baby now." She tugged at the strand of hair, but didn't push it away from her face.

"No. I'm not," Scotty said firmly. "I'm not! Hear me? I'm *not!*" He held himself back. He could feel his anger taking over, feel it turn to rage. He felt himself going out of control.

Why didn't she listen to him? Why was she doing this to him?

He wanted to hit something. He wanted to hit *her*.

He closed his fists, then opened them again.

Get control, get control, get control, he repeated to himself.

"I'm not good enough for you?" she asked forlornly, looking up at him, staring into his eyes with her big, brown, sad eyes. "Is that it?"

"No, that's not it," he said coldly. "We had one date. Now it's over. I already told you." He looked down the street, afraid he might see the Pontiac heading home with Denny and his mother.

"You're hurting my feelings," Shannon wailed, tears running down her puffy cheeks. "You're hurting my feelings, Scotty. I'm getting very upset."

"Don't be upset," he said, feeling very helpless, nervously watching the street. "It was just *one* date, Shannon. Be fair — okay?"

"My brothers won't like this," she said, wiping her wet cheeks with her hand.

"What?"

"My brothers," she said, sniffling. "They don't like it when people aren't nice to me."

She's threatening me, Scotty thought angrily. I

don't believe this. She's threatening me with her three monster brothers.

"I'm trying to be nice to you," he said. "I'm trying to be honest. Okay? I think you should forget about me. I think — "

He stopped. He saw his mom's car turn the corner, Denny beside her in the front seat.

"Listen, Shannon — you've got to go — *now*." He grabbed her arms and pulled her to her feet.

"Let go of me!" she cried, struggling away from him.

"My mom is almost here," he said frantically. "You've got to go."

"But I want to meet Mom," she insisted, following Scotty's gaze to the street. "I think it's time I met Mom, don't you?"

"No!" The car was half a block away. "Listen, Shannon — go now and I'll call you tonight," he offered, tugging at the sleeve of her windbreaker.

"Huh? Really?" Her whole face brightened.

"Yeah. I'll call you. After dinner. We'll have a long talk," he said. "Just go. Now. Please!"

"Okay, baby. Call me tonight," she said, smiling for the first time. She started toward the driveway, but he grabbed her and pulled her the other way, to the side of the house.

"Go that way. Call you tonight. Promise," he said.

She ran off, stopping once to look back at him uncertainly, then disappeared through the hedges to the street just as his mom's car pulled up the driveway.

"AAAAAAGH!" Scotty screamed, letting out only a little of his anger and frustration.

What am I going to *do*?

Furiously, he picked up his bookbag and heaved it toward the front door. He hadn't meant to throw it as hard as he did. It crashed into the storm door, shattering the glass.

"No!" he screamed. "Oh, no!"

He could hear the car doors slam around back, could hear Denny's high-pitched voice repeating, "I'm hungry! I'm hungry!"

Scotty started trudging up the driveway to join them when something caught his eye. A shadow. A large one. Moving quickly from the side of the house, along the hedges toward the street.

"Hey — " Scotty called out.

He saw a man, a very large man, wearing a long raincoat, appear between the hedges, then quickly duck out of view.

"Hey — " Scotty called again, at first not believing his eyes. He stood frozen on the driveway, more surprised than frightened, staring at the hedges that were now still.

Someone was here, Scotty thought.

Someone was watching Shannon and me.

And then he realized. It must have been one of Shannon's brothers. "My brothers are enormous," she had told him, and this guy, even seen from behind, seen in a split second, was certainly enormous, his raincoat billowing behind him as he ran.

"My brothers don't like it when people aren't nice to me," Shannon had said. It was definitely meant as a threat. And one of the three hulks was standing there the whole time, standing in the shadows at the side of the house, watching, listening.

Maybe the whole family is crazy, Scotty thought, chilled by the thought.

What am I going to do?

Trying to conceal his troubled feelings, he hurried around to the back where his mother was struggling with the back door, several shopping bags in her hands. "Scotty," she called out, "are you just getting home?"

"Yeah," he lied. He was getting used to lying.

"I'm hungry," Denny whined.

"I know, I know," Mrs. Singleton groaned.

"The front door is broken," Scotty said. "The glass on the storm door, it's shattered."

"What?" His mother's mouth dropped open. "How?"

Scotty shrugged. "I don't know. I saw it as I came up the drive. Looks like somebody threw something at it."

"Well, maybe we'll just remove it or put the screen back up," she said, frowning. "A new storm door is not in my budget." She brightened and held up the shopping bags. "Especially after the money I spent on this."

"What's that?" Scotty asked.

"I'm hungry," Denny shouted.

She pushed open the door, and they went inside. "It's the new outfit I bought for Saturday. You know. For the Junior Chamber of Commerce."

"You bought a special dress for that?" Scotty asked. He started to open the refrigerator, but Denny got there first, darting between his legs to win the race.

"Of course," his mother said, smiling as she held up the silky chartreuse dress to show him. "It's a special day, isn't it? I had to buy the perfect dress in honor of the perfect couple. I'm just so proud of you and Lora. Everyone is."

"I'm not," Denny said. "I'm hungry."

In his room after dinner, Scotty tried to concentrate on his government studies text. But he couldn't read an entire paragraph without thinking about Shannon. And about her brother, spying on them.

Slamming the book shut in exasperation, he reached for the phone. I'm going to call Shannon, he decided, and tell her once and for all that I don't want to go out with her again, that I don't want her to ever call me again.

But then he pulled his hand back. No. I've already told her. A hundred times. I promised to call her tonight. But I'm not going to. And when she sees that I'm not calling, she'll realize that I'm serious.

And then her enormous brother will beat me to a pulp, he thought.

He stared at the phone. No. No way. I'm not going to call her.

He opened the textbook again and shuffled through to find his place. He still hadn't found it when the phone rang.

He felt his heart skip a beat. He jumped to his feet.

It rang a second time. A third.

He didn't want to pick it up, but no one downstairs seemed to be answering it. "Hello?" he said softly, timidly.

"Where were you, man?" a familiar voice asked without any greeting.

"Bender?"

"Yeah, it's me. Where were you?"

Scotty was so relieved to hear Bender's voice, he could barely hear what his friend was saying. "What do you mean?"

"Where were you? Why weren't you at practice?" Bender asked impatiently.

"Oh, no!" Scotty slapped his forehead. He had been so obsessed with Shannon that he'd forgotten all about his after-school football practice.

"Coach Hawkins was really steamed," Bender said. "He gave Berman extra time. Had him passing all afternoon."

Berman was the second-string quarterback. He wasn't bad. Scotty knew if he slipped up, Berman would take his place in an instant.

"Tell me Berman wasn't any good," Scotty pleaded.

"He wasn't bad," Bender said. "He's really got an arm. He can heave the ball a mile. I think Hawkins was impressed."

"You're a real pal," Scotty said sarcastically. "I *asked* you to tell me he wasn't any good!"

"So where were you?" Bender asked.

"I was . . . busy," Scotty said, struggling unsuccessfully to think of a good excuse. "I had to do some things . . . for my mom."

There was a long silence at the other end. Scotty knew that Bender wasn't buying his story.

"You've been acting kind of weird lately," Bender said finally. "Who was that girl you were talking to?"

"Girl?"

"Yeah. You know. Real little. With the wild, red hair."

"Oh. I don't know her name. She has a locker next to mine, that's all," Scotty told him.

I'm lying to everyone now, he thought.

He had a sudden strong urge to tell Bender everything, but held back. Bender would just make a joke, Scotty thought. Or he might tell someone else. I've got to handle this on my own.

He knew he couldn't take a chance. What if word somehow got back to Lora?

"You sure everything's okay?" Bender asked.

"Yeah. Fine," Scotty said. "See you tomorrow, man."

He hung up and reached for the textbook. "How

am I ever going to read this?" he asked himself aloud.

The phone rang again.

Bender almost always called back with something he'd forgotten. Scotty picked up the receiver. "Hello?"

"Baby, you didn't call." Shannon's whispery voice reverberated in his ear. He could feel his neck muscles tighten.

His entire body tensed. He couldn't hold back his anger any longer. "I didn't call you — and I'm *never* going to call you!" he screamed.

He could hear a sharp intake of breath followed by a low whimper on the other end. He didn't care if he hurt her now. He was too angry to care.

"I don't *want* to call you, Shannon!" he cried. "I don't want to *see* you! We're not going out. Not ever. Hear? I don't want to go out with you."

He took a breath. His heart was pounding. His mouth was dry. There was no sound at all on the other end of the line.

"Leave me alone," he continued. "I mean it. Leave me alone, Shannon. Don't call me again." He slammed the receiver down without waiting for any kind of reply.

"There," he said aloud and reached for his textbook. "That's done."

# Chapter 11

Scotty felt good the next morning, having slept well, a peaceful, dreamless sleep. Lora called while he was eating breakfast. He was happy to hear her voice.

"I've been thinking about your birthday," she said.

"Huh?" He swallowed a mouthful of Frosted Flakes. "My birthday is two weeks away."

"So? How shall we celebrate?" she asked. "Should we have a party or something?"

"A party? No. I — " He realized he wasn't awake enough to discuss this. "Can we talk about this later?"

Lora always did this to him. She couldn't bear to be thinking about something alone. If she had something on her mind, she had to call no matter what time it was and make him think about it, too.

"Want to meet after school?" she asked.

"No. I've got football practice," he said. A heavy feeling of dread sank through his body. He knew he was going to be chewed out by Coach Hawkins this afternoon for missing practice. "How about lunch?"

"Okay," she agreed. "The usual place. And think about your birthday, okay?"

"Okay," he said, and hung up. He gulped down the last spoonful of the sweet cereal, tilted the bowl to his mouth to drink the milk, then started to look for Denny. "Denny — where are you? We're going to be late."

Denny came limping into the room, one sneaker on, one off. "I've got a knot in my shoe," he whined, handing the shoe to Scotty.

How does he do it? Scotty wondered, shaking his head. How does he get a knot in his shoe *every* morning?

Scotty dropped Denny off at the elementary school, then continued on to the high school a block away. When he turned the corner and started down the corridor to his locker, he was relieved to see that Shannon wasn't waiting for him there.

He smiled, feeling better, feeling the sense of dread begin to lift. He locked up his coat, then, carrying the books he'd need that morning, talked with friends until the bell for homeroom rang. Shannon was nowhere to be seen.

After fourth period, he met Lora at their usual meeting place outside the lunchroom. "You got a haircut!" he exclaimed, immediately noticing her new, short hairdo.

"Do you like it?" she asked, patting it in exaggerated fashion like a primping movie star. "I wanted to look nice for Saturday."

"Are we really going to show up for that thing Saturday?" he asked, rolling his eyes.

"No. You're going to turn down the five hundred dollars," she replied dryly. "What do you need money for?"

"Okay, okay. We're doing it," he said. "But it's going to be so bogus."

"It's only a few hours of your life, Scotty," Lora said, pulling him into the lunchroom. "What could be so terrible?"

As they ate their sandwiches, Scotty kept alert, looking for Shannon. But she never appeared.

He didn't see her all day. Driving home after football practice, he wondered if she'd be waiting for him on the front stoop.

The afternoon was warm for November, but gray clouds were rolling in, bringing a chill to the air. The bare trees seemed to shiver along the sides of the street as he turned onto his block and then pulled up the drive.

He glanced at the front stoop, then moved his eyes around the front yard.

No Shannon. She wasn't there.

"All right!" he shouted happily inside the car.

He jumped out of the car and stretched. He suddenly felt very light, as if a heavy weight had been lifted from him.

Finally.

I finally made her understand.

Carrying his backpack by the straps, he started to the back door. But he stopped on the walk, suddenly remembering Ernie, his snake, and lowered the backpack to the ground.

I'd better check on Ernie, he thought. I forgot all about him yesterday.

Walking quickly, he headed to the side of the garage. Two fat, gray squirrels scampered along the fence at the back of the yard, kicking up the dead leaves as they ran.

When the cage came into view, Scotty stopped. And gaped.

The screened cage top was off, lying on the ground beside the cage.

Had Ernie escaped?

Scotty started to run. How had the top come off? It was too heavy to be blown off by the wind. Someone had to have *taken* it off.

But — wait. The snake hadn't escaped. It was still in the cage.

Yes. As Scotty came up to it, he could see Ernie on the glass cage floor.

"Ernie, what's — ?" Scotty started to say. But his mouth dropped open in horror, and he never finished his greeting.

The snake, he saw, had been cut in two.

# Chapter 12

"You have to break up with her, baby."

Shannon called him right after dinner. He was upstairs, pacing back and forth in his room, unable to get the picture of his pet snake out of his mind. Ernie had been sliced cleanly across the middle, cut into two almost-perfect halves.

Scotty was standing right next to the phone when it rang. Startled, he uttered a short cry, then picked up the receiver before the first ring had ended. "Hello?"

"You have to break up with her, baby."

Shannon didn't even bother to say hello. Her voice was as whispery as ever, but there was a hard, determined tone to it, an edge Scotty had never heard before.

"Shannon — did you kill my snake?" he asked angrily, balling his free hand into a tight fist.

"You have to break up with her. You *have* to."

"Did you? Did you kill my snake? Answer me!"

"You have to break up with her, Scotty."

Scotty made the fist tighter and tighter until his hand ached with pain. Slowly, he relaxed his hand. His voice trembled from anger as he spoke. "Stop repeating that and answer my question."

"You've hurt me, baby," she said, her little-girl voice returning. "Please don't make me hurt you more."

"More? What do you mean by *more*, Shannon?" he screamed. "You're admitting it? You're admitting that you did it?"

"Come over tonight, and we'll talk about it," she whispered.

"What? Are you serious — ?"

"Come over," she repeated playfully. "There's no one here but me. I'm very lonely, baby."

"Shannon — I — I'm going to call the police," he said, surprising himself. He didn't know if he was serious or not. He hadn't really thought about it. The words just popped out.

"The police?" her voice grew even tinier. Then, to his surprise, she giggled. "My brothers wouldn't like that."

"I don't care about your brothers," he declared. "I've decided. I'm calling the police."

There was a pause. Then she said softly, "No, you're not. Because then Lora would find out. Wouldn't she? And her parents. I'd have to tell everyone then, wouldn't I? Everyone would know about you and me, baby."

"Now, wait — " He didn't know what to say next. Shannon was right, of course. There was no way he could go to the police. If Lora found out, she'd break up with him. He'd lose her. He'd lose . . . everything.

Besides, he had no way of proving that Shannon killed the snake. The police would laugh at him, wouldn't listen to him at all.

"Come over, baby," she urged. "Stop being so silly."

"I'm never coming over," he said slowly, speaking each word clearly and distinctly. "Hear me? I'm never coming over. And if you call me, or threaten me, or do something else to me — *anything* — I'll call the police, Shannon. I really will."

He hung up the phone and realized he was trembling all over.

A loud knock on the bedroom door made him jump.

The door swung open, and Denny came skipping in, a big grin on his face. "What do you want?" Scotty snapped, not meaning to sound so harsh, trying to calm down, not wanting Denny to see how upset he was.

"Can I ask you a favor?" Denny asked, fiddling with the homework papers on Scotty's desk.

"Yeah. I guess."

"It's a pretty big favor," Denny said.

"That's okay. Go ahead and ask."

"It's kind of a *really* big favor," Denny said reluctantly.

"Denny — " Scotty snapped angrily.

"Could I borrow Ernie?" Denny asked. "We're

having a science show-and-tell, and I told everyone I was bringing a snake."

"No. Sorry," Scotty said quickly. He pictured the snake, lying so still and straight, cut into two halves, its insides pouring out onto the glass cage floor.

"Why not?" Denny asked angrily, shoving Scotty's papers across the desk.

"Ernie escaped," Scotty said, thinking quickly. "I . . . uh . . . didn't get a chance to tell you."

"He escaped?" Denny stared up at him, his face filled with surprise.

"Yeah. The lid came off somehow. It was off when I came home, and Ernie was gone."

Actually, Scotty had lifted the two snake halves into a plastic trash bag and buried the trash bag in the dirt behind the garage.

"You mean, Ernie is out in the backyard somewhere?" Denny asked, looking upset.

"I don't think so," Scotty told him, putting a reassuring hand on his shoulder. "I searched all over for him. I think he probably went to the woods. Snakes like it in the woods."

Denny wanted to talk about it more, but Scotty had homework to do and guided him out of the room. That night, Scotty couldn't get to sleep. The picture of his pet, sliced so neatly, so coldly, so cruelly, wouldn't fade from his mind.

It was already dark when football practice ended the next afternoon. The sky was inky black with eerie gray streaks of clouds, ghostly images floating low overhead. The air was cold and damp.

"It could snow for the Madison game Friday night," Scotty said, zipping his down jacket up to the top, ducking his head into the collar for protection against the damp wind.

Bender pulled his Hard Rock Cafe cap low on his forehead as he loped along beside Scotty. His glasses reflected the light from a street lamp. "I guess snow would help us and hurt them," he said thoughtfully.

"How come?" Scotty asked.

Bender shrugged. "No reason. Just trying to sound as if I know something." He laughed. Scotty punched him on the shoulder.

They turned the corner onto Scotty's street. The wind seemed to blow into their faces no matter which direction they walked. Despite the cold, Bender had his down vest unzipped.

"What are you and Lora doing after the game?" Bender asked.

"I don't know," Scotty replied. "You think Hawkins will get off my case before Friday?"

"You know Hawkins," Bender said. "He thinks it's good psychology to make you mad. Thinks it gets you fired up."

"It only gets me mad," Scotty said. "I didn't play so bad today."

As they reached the corner, Bender pretended to walk right into the mailbox. He hit the mailbox hard with his whole body and fell back onto the sidewalk. Bender was always doing things like that, walking into trees, falling down. It usually cracked Scotty up, but he didn't feel like laughing today.

Scotty helped Bender up. "I hope you throw better blocks than that Friday night," he said.

He looked up and saw Shannon standing on the sidewalk in front of them. The streetlight above cast her in an eerie green glow. She was wearing the same plastic windbreaker. Her jeans were tucked into knee-high black boots. In the pale light, she looked frail and tiny, old-fashioned-looking with her long hair flowing freely behind her shoulders, like a Victorian painting of an angel.

"Hi, Scotty," she said softly, smiling with pleasure at the shock on his face.

"Shannon, I warned you — " Scotty said, looking at Bender, who was staring wide-eyed at Shannon, nervously readjusting his cap.

"Why didn't you come to see me last night?" Shannon asked, still smiling, stepping closer.

Scotty didn't reply. He could feel his muscles tense. He was too angry to be embarrassed, but he wished Bender weren't there.

"Hi," Bender said to Shannon. "I'm Scotty's good-looking friend. David Bender. But you can call me Bender like everyone else."

Shannon didn't look at Bender, didn't acknowledge that he was there. "You hurt my feelings, baby," she said to Scotty in her little-girl voice. "Why didn't you come over?"

Scotty's face was frozen in anger. He refused to

reply, hoping his silence would force her to retreat, to disappear.

"Hey — if you two want to be alone . . ." Bender said, casting a meaningful look at Scotty.

"No," Scotty replied quickly. "Let's go, man. I don't know this girl."

"She seems to know you — *baby!*" Bender cracked. He smiled at Shannon, who continued to ignore him.

"Why won't you be nice to me, Scotty?" Shannon asked, her tiny voice barely carrying over the wind. "I was very nice to you. Remember?"

"Wow!" Bender exclaimed.

"Let's go, man," Scotty said, avoiding Shannon's stare.

He started to walk past her, but she stepped into his path, blocking his way. "Don't go, Scotty."

Still ignoring her, he pulled to the right, walking fast. "Let's go, Bender," he insisted.

But Shannon grabbed his arm with both hands, as if making a high, shoulder tackle. "Wait, baby."

"Hey — let go!" Scotty protested.

Shannon slid her hands down the sleeve of Scotty's jacket and squeezed his hand between hers. Scotty saw Bender behind them, staring in disbelief. He tried to pull his hand away from her, but her grip was surprisingly strong.

"Don't go, baby," she pleaded, tears running down her cheeks.

"Come on, Shannon — let go of me!" Scotty cried.

"You two want to Indian wrestle?" Bender suggested. "How about two out of three? I'm betting on *her*!"

"Let go. I don't want to hold hands!" Scotty yelled, surprised by how strong this frail-looking little girl was.

"Don't go. Please — stay with me!" Tears were streaming down her face. "Don't make me hurt you, Scotty. I don't want to hurt you."

As she said this, she grabbed two of his fingers with one hand, the other two fingers with her other hand.

"Hey — !" Scotty cried, struggling to free himself.

But she was so strong, so surprisingly strong.

And then, her face distorted with fury, Shannon pulled down hard, yanking the fingers in two different directions.

At first, Scotty didn't feel anything.

He heard the loud *crack*.

It was loud enough for all three of them to hear it.

He screamed as the pain coursed up his arm, then shot through his entire body. Everything went red, then white. He dropped to his knees. He had never felt such pain. His entire right side throbbed. Gasping for breath, he held his arm close to his body, as if trying to protect it, to squeeze away the pain.

When Scotty focused again, he saw Bender, looking pale, his mouth open, gulping air, his eyes wide behind the black-framed glasses, gaping at Shannon with shock and disbelief.

Shannon had stepped back under the eerie green light of the street lamp. She seemed to be shocked by what she had done. Wet tears slid down her cheeks. She tugged at the sides of her hair with both hands.

"Shannon — my hand — " Scotty managed to cry out in a terrified voice he didn't recognize. He held the injured hand up by the wrist with his left hand.

"I'm so sorry, baby," she cried, shaking her head. "I'm so, so sorry." Then she turned and ran, her windbreaker flapping noisily behind her.

"My hand — " Scotty called after her. He turned his gaze on Bender. "It's — it's broken!"

# Chapter 13

Behind him in the bleachers, Glenview fans cheered and shouted. Scotty leaned forward on the bench to get a better view. On the first play from scrimmage, Berman went back to pass. He looked left, then right.

Too long. You're taking too long, Scotty thought. You're going to eat the ball.

He was right. Berman was swarmed by three gold-and-green-uniformed Madison players. He hit the ground hard, sacked, and they piled on top of him.

The crowd in the bleachers groaned and then grew quiet.

Scotty turned downfield to see the cheerleaders. They were facing the crowd, clapping in rhythm, shouting a "Go, Tigers" cheer. Lora stood in the center, leaping high in her short, green-and-white-skirted cheerleader uniform. She looks great, Scotty thought.

Shifting the heavy cast on his hand, he turned back to the game in time to see a handoff to Barker, stopped at the line of scrimmage. Third down. The Madison players seemed really fired-up. A cheer went up from the Madison supporters on the other side of the field.

Scotty groaned as the next play began, and Berman fumbled the snap from center. Luckily a Glenview player fell on the ball. But now it was fourth down. The Tigers had to punt.

I should be in there, Scotty thought, pounding his knee with the heavy, white cast over his hand. He looked down at the cast, feeling his anger starting to rise.

But he realized he was more angry at himself than at Shannon. I let everyone down, he thought. I let Coach Hawkins down. I let the team down.

He looked past the bench toward the cheerleaders. Lora had turned around to watch the punt. Her short hair glowed golden under the bright white stadium lights. She turned and looked back at him, her smile momentarily fading. Their eyes met. He waved at her with the cast. She turned back to the field.

I let Lora down, too, Scotty thought glumly. And her parents. And everyone else who believes in me.

The punt was short. The Glenview supporters in the bleachers behind the team bench groaned. Madison would be starting out on the Glenview forty-five.

*"Dee-fense! Dee-fense!"* the cheerleaders were chanting.

After Shannon broke Scotty's hand, Bender had taken him to the emergency room at Glenview General. On the way, Scotty had to explain a little bit about Shannon, after first making Bender swear to total secrecy.

"She's been after me for weeks," he lied, feeling bad, feeling guilty about all the lying he'd had to do. But what choice did he have? "She calls me, and comes to my house, and follows me everywhere," he told Bender. "She wants me to go out with her, but of course I won't. She's crazy. Just plain crazy."

"You've got to call the police," Bender urged.

"No, I can't," Scotty said, resting his head on the seat in Bender's car, grimacing as his hand throbbed with pain. "The police won't do anything."

"But she broke your hand, man!" Bender exclaimed, nearly driving through a stoplight. "That's assault, isn't it?"

"She'd just say it was an accident," Scotty said softly, afraid to tell Bender the real reason he didn't want to call the police. Afraid to tell Bender any of the real story.

"Well, at least you can call her parents," Bender suggested, turning into the hospital driveway. "Let them know what their daughter is doing. Tell them she's got to be put on a leash or something."

"Yeah. That's a good idea," Scotty had said thoughtfully.

Bender was right, he realized. He *could* call Shannon's parents and tell them that Shannon was driving him crazy. Or maybe even talk to one of her brothers.

The whole family couldn't be as weird as she is — could they?

He told everyone, including his mother, that he had slammed his hand in a car door. Lora had been terribly sympathetic. She called him a clumsy clod, but she said it in a nice way. Coach Hawkins hadn't been as nice.

That night, trying to get to sleep, Scotty kept hearing the crack his fingers made as Shannon pulled them in different directions. The pain had subsided, but his hand itched constantly, and of course, he couldn't scratch it.

The next morning, he tried calling her house at lunchtime, hoping to catch someone home while Shannon was in school. He had carefully rehearsed what he was going to say, repeating it endlessly in his mind. He was going to tell them that he was a friend of Shannon's and that as a friend, he was calling to say that she needed help, that he was very worried about her. He was going to tell them that she had been calling him constantly, following him around, and threatening violence.

It was the truth, after all.

If they weren't sympathetic, he was going to threaten to call the police. He hoped he wouldn't have to do that. He wanted to stop Shannon. But he didn't want to get her so upset that she'd do something drastic, like call Lora.

Despite his endless rehearsal of what he was going to say, his heart was pounding as he punched in her phone number. The phone rang and rang, but no one answered.

He tried again right after school. Again, no one was home.

That night, he dialed her house again, hoping that one of her parents or brothers would answer. But he immediately recognized Shannon's breathy "Hello?" and slammed down the phone.

Her "hello" had sounded so eager, so hopeful, that for a moment Scotty had felt sorry for her. But then he glanced at his hand in the big, white cast and rememberd that the football season was over for him, as were his chances of being named all-state, and he felt only anger.

He tried calling three more times during the week. But Shannon had answered each time, and each time he had immediately hung up. Finally he gave up the idea, and his carefully rehearsed speech faded from his mind.

Now, here he was on Friday night, sitting on the team bench in his street clothes, balancing his heavy cast on his lap, feeling terribly guilty and terribly sorry for himself at the same time, watching the Tigers lose to a team he knew he could have beaten.

The final score was 21–3.

As the team trudged to the locker room, Scotty

stayed on the bench, slumping low, feeling chilled by the night air, staring across the now-empty field as people made their way out of the stadium.

"Hey, man, we missed you," Bender said, standing over Scotty, his helmet in his hand, his hair matted down on his head, sweat covering his forehead despite the cold night air.

"Yeah, well . . ." Scotty stared across the field uncomfortably.

"Only one more game," Bender said, breathing hard. "That girl still bothering you?"

"No," Scotty told him, still avoiding his glance. "I haven't seen her all week."

"Hey — that's great!" Bender said. "That's terrific."

"You haven't told anyone about her?" Scotty asked nervously.

"No. No way," Bender replied, looking hurt that Scotty would ask that question. "You meeting Lora?"

"Yeah. She's getting changed. Then we're going to go get something to eat. Want to come?"

"No. Thanks. I'm going to hang out with some of the guys on the team. Later, okay? I've got to get changed." He jogged off toward the locker room.

Scotty stayed on the bench for a while, staring at the shiny green turf, thinking about Shannon and about Lora. He was startled when the stadium lights went out, casting everything in darkness.

Standing up, he turned to see Lora watching him from the cinder track at the edge of the field. "Hi," she called, waving. She had changed into maroon corduroys. Her shearling coat was open, revealing a white, crew-neck sweater. "What on earth are you doing?"

"Nothing much," he said, hurrying over to her. "Just waiting for you."

"You were sitting there feeling sorry for yourself," she said, taking his arm and giving him a quick kiss on the cheek. Her nose and lips felt hot against his cold face. "Admit it."

"Maybe a little," he confessed, smiling guiltily.

"Well, I have some news that should cheer you up," she said, holding tightly onto his arm as they walked to the parking lot.

"The Junior Chamber of Commerce disbanded, and we don't have to go to that stupid thing tomorrow?" he joked.

She slapped his arm, accidentally hitting the top of the cast. "Oh. Sorry. No. My news is that Daddy has decided to take on an intern for the summer at his firm, and you're it."

"Huh?"

"You heard me, Scotty. You can work as an intern there this summer, and he'll even pay you. Not a lot, but it'll give you some spending money for when we're at Princeton in the fall."

"Wow! That's great!" Scotty exclaimed, brightening.

"Am I cheering you up?" she asked, clinging to him, pulling the shearling coat together with her free hand.

"Yeah. You're doing a great job," Scotty said sincerely.

"Well, here's more," she said, grinning at him. "Daddy says you can come up to the Cape with us in August and stay for two whole weeks."

Scotty stopped and turned to her. "Really?" He hadn't looked forward to August. He knew Lora would spend the whole month up at the Cape with her family, and he wouldn't get to see her. "That's awesome!" he declared.

"Stick with me, kid," she said playfully. "I'll show you a good time."

"August is a long way away," he complained. "It's only November."

"Hey — I'm trying to cheer you up," she said, laughing. "Give me a break."

"Please — don't say *break*," he groaned, holding up his cast.

She gave him a playful shove. He reached for her, but then stopped short as the parking lot came into view.

There, leaning casually against the hood of his Pontiac, was Shannon. She was wearing the same outfit as the last time he'd seen her — jeans tucked into high black boots, the plastic windbreaker, which she always seemed to wear no matter how cold it was.

Did she see him?

No. Not yet. She was looking toward the other stadium exit.

Looking past her, trying to decide what to do, Scotty's eyes bulged in surprise. Someone else was standing a few cars down, hiding in shadows, keeping low behind a black Jeep.

It was the large man Scotty had seen running along the hedges from his yard. Shannon's enormous brother!

A wave of fear shot through him. Why had Shannon brought her brother? Why was he hiding in the shadows a few cars away from Shannon?

She had already broken his hand. Wasn't that enough? Now, what did she and her huge brother have planned for him?

"Uh . . . can we take your car?" Scotty asked Lora, trying to make his voice sound normal.

Lora looked at him, confused. "Huh? Why?"

"Uh . . . mine doesn't have much gas," he lied.

"Well, okay. I'm parked on the street," she said, still clinging to his arm. "Your muscles are all tight," she said, squeezing his bicep through his jacket. "How come you're so tense?"

"You just excite me," he cracked, leading her quickly in the other direction, away from the parking lot.

"Hey — what's the rush?" Lora protested.

"I'm hungry," he lied. "Let's go get some burgers."

Did Shannon see me? he wondered. What is she doing there? Is she going to wait there all night?

He turned back to see.

"Oh!" He gaped in horror as he saw the flames shoot out from the front seat of his car.

Still standing a little in front of the car, Shannon stared at him, hands on her hips, just stood and stared, as still as a statue, bathed in the yellow glow of the fire.

# Chapter 14

"I have to tell you something, Shannon, and you have to listen to me," Scotty said, softly, seriously.

She tugged at a strand of her hair, but didn't reply.

They were sitting on the sofa in her living room, its cushions worn and sagging. The only light came from a dim bulb in the back hallway.

She edged closer to him, her face covered in shadow. He could smell the sweet, flowery perfume she was wearing.

"Will you listen to me?" he asked softly. "I have the feeling that you do not listen to me, Shannon."

She leaned forward, bent her head, and brushed her hair against his cheek. It sent a shiver of excitement through him.

"Shannon — ?" He really wanted to talk to her, to communicate with her. He had to set things straight, once and for all.

She pressed her head against his shoulder, a tender gesture.

"Shannon — ?"

"You hurt me, Scotty," she whispered.

He leaned away, tried to get some room between them. "That's what I want to talk to you about," he said.

The ceiling creaked. What was that sound? Footsteps? Was someone walking around upstairs?

"You hurt me," she repeated. She raised her head and stared at him, her dark eyes burning into his. "And when I get hurt, I hurt back," she told him, still whispering.

"That's what I wanted to talk to you about," he said, edging away, trying to back away from the warmth of her, the fragrance of her perfume. "You see, I can't see you. Ever again."

She stared at him, her face expressionless, beautiful in the dim light.

"I know we had something really special," Scotty said. "But you have to understand that it's over. I really can't see you."

She remained silent. The only sounds now were the creaking of the ceiling, her soft, rhythmic breathing, the insistent pounding of his heart.

"Do you understand?" he asked, raising his voice for the first time.

"Let me see your hand," she said, reaching for him.

He pulled his arm away. "You broke my hand, Shannon. Why do you want to see it?"

"Let me see the other hand, baby. I want to tell your future."

"No," he insisted. "I'm *telling* you the future. I cannot see you again."

Her lips puckered into a childish pout.

"Do you understand? Do you finally understand?" Scotty demanded.

"I'm very hurt," she said, still pouting. "You have hurt me a lot, Scotty. And my brothers don't like it when I'm hurt."

As she said this, the floorboards creaked and groaned. The room filled with dark figures, moving quickly through the shadows, large figures, lumbering noisily.

A light went on overhead. Three enormous men stood in front of the couch, glaring at Scotty. Even though they were indoors, all three were wearing long trench coats with wide lapels. All three had round, red faces, topped with short-cropped white-blond hair.

"My brothers don't like people who hurt me, Scotty," Shannon said in her whispery voice, speaking tonelessly, without any expression at all.

"Now, wait — " Scotty started, suddenly terrified. He looked up at the three identical brothers looming menacingly over him, so big, so muscular, their faces locked on him, seething in silent anger.

"Get him," one of the brothers said, raising his arms as if to perform a stranglehold.

"Get him," the others grunted.

Scotty uttered a low cry and shrank back on the sofa as the three enormous men circled the couch, then closed in on him.

# Chapter 15

The phone was ringing.

He stirred, pushed himself up, and squinting against the morning light, looked for Shannon's brothers.

The phone rang again.

"It was a dream," he said aloud, his throat still clogged with sleep.

Of *course* it was a dream. An ugly, frightening dream. But just a dream.

He picked up the phone and cleared his throat. "Hello?"

The dream lingered in his mind. He expected to hear Shannon at the other end.

"Hi, did I wake you?"

"Lora?" He was relieved to hear her voice. He glanced at the clock. Ten-twenty.

"Who were you expecting?" she asked teasingly. "Your mystery girl?"

Her joke sent a shock wave down the back of his neck.

Did she know something? Did she mean something by that?

Of course not.

Don't go completely mental, Scotty, he scolded himself.

"I guess I slept late," he said uncertainly. "What's happening?"

"That was so horrible with the car last night, I just wondered how you were," she said.

"I'm okay, I guess. Mom took it pretty well," he told her, remembering the night before with a shudder. It all came back to him in a series of ugly pictures flashing before his eyes: the flames licking up from the car, Shannon seeming to disappear into thin air along with her mysterious brother, Scotty running to the car, the fire trucks, the hoses, the crowd of onlookers.

"Did the firemen figure out what caused the fire?" Lora asked.

"Yeah. They think it was a match," Scotty told her. "They think someone came out from the game, lit up a cigarette, and tossed the match into my front seat. It was so bogus of me to leave the window open."

Of course, Scotty knew that wasn't how his car was set on fire. He knew that Shannon had done it. He could still see her standing there staring at him and Lora as the flames grew higher and higher behind her.

I've got to talk to Shannon, he thought. I've got to make her see that this all has to stop.

He glanced down at his broken hand. It itched like crazy. He banged the cast against the wall, but it didn't help.

This all has to stop. It *has* to!

"Mom's making her famous Belgian waffles for breakfast," Lora said.

"Is *that* what smells so good?" he joked, sniffing loudly into the receiver.

"Why don't you hurry up and get dressed and come over for breakfast?" Lora suggested.

"Well, no I — "

"Don't say no," she interrupted. "Say yes."

"But I'm going to see you in a few hours at this stupid Junior Chamber of Commerce thing."

"Oh, I see," she replied sharply. "And seeing me twice in one day would be too much for you, huh?"

"Okay. I'll be there in fifteen minutes," he quickly agreed. "Don't eat all the waffles before I get there."

"Me?!" she cried with exaggerated indignation. "You pig! I'm not the one who swallows the waffles whole! I wouldn't touch your stupid waffles!"

"Don't yell," he said softly.

"Why not?" she screamed.

"Because I have a broken hand."

She laughed. "You're weird, Singleton. Hurry over, okay? I want to show you the dress I'm wearing this afternoon. Wait till you see it. It's a riot.

It looks like something my grandmother would wear."

"Can't wait," he said sarcastically. He faked a loud yawn.

"Hey — be a good sport about this afternoon," she said.

"Huh?"

"Be a good boy at the Autumn Ball and maybe I'll buy you a balloon."

"See you," he said, and hung up.

When he came downstairs, his mother was on the phone with the insurance company about the car. "Be home in a few hours," he whispered. She looked up, concentrating on her conversation, and gave him a quick wave. "But I need a car right away. Can you get me a replacement?" she was saying.

Feeling guilty, Scotty headed out the front door and began walking to Lora's house, only four blocks away. It was a clear, crisp day. The sky was bright blue and cloudless.

Much too nice a day to be cooped up with the Junior Chamber of Commerce, he thought unhappily.

The Belgian waffles cheered him up a little. Mrs. DeMarco kept pouring more batter on the waffle iron, bringing replacements to the table so fast Scotty could barely keep up. Finally, feeling stuffed, he begged her to stop. "I won't fit into my jacket this afternoon!" he told her.

"Speaking of that hideous jacket," said Lora, getting up from the table, "come see my dress." She grabbed his hand and pulled him to her room.

"Hey, what's wrong with my jacket?" he asked, pretending to be offended. They'd had this conversation before.

"It looks just like a horse blanket I saw at the riding stable last week," Lora told him.

"Yeah, but what's *wrong* with it?" he joked.

They both laughed. She closed the door to her room, threw her arms around his neck, and kissed him. "You always make me happy," she said.

Normally he'd feel happy, too. But this morning, every nice thing Lora said just made him feel guilty.

She pulled the dress out of the closet. He agreed that it was weird-looking. It was a blue sheath dress made of some sort of shiny material. "I'm going to look like a grownup," she said, holding it up in front of her. "And you're going to look like a horse!"

"Lay off my jacket," he grumbled, making a sour face.

She whinnied at him, doing a pretty fair imitation of a horse.

"Give me a break, Lora!" he cried.

She whinnied again, laughing. He started to chase her around the room. Laughing, they stumbled out into the hall.

"It's still early," she said, taking his hand. "We don't have to be there till two. Come out in the backyard for a while."

She led him out through the sliding glass doors. They crossed the terrace, stopped to look at the covered swimming pool, then started walking slowly, arm in arm, down the wide, sloping lawn.

"Daddy's real excited that you're going to intern at his place this summer," she said, taking a deep breath of the fresh, sweet-smelling air.

"Not as excited as I am," Scotty told her.

"I think it's real cute how he's kind of adopted you," Lora said chirpily. "I think he always wanted a son. Instead he got me."

"You're all right," Scotty said, grinning.

"Thanks a bunch," she said sarcasatically, giving him a playful shove.

She stopped suddenly. "What's that?"

Scotty followed her stare. There was a small, dark object lying in the grass near the wooden fence.

"That's odd," Lora said. "Let's see what it is."

As they stepped closer, walking quickly over the wet grass, the object came into view. It was a black cap, lying upside down.

"Hey — isn't that the Raiders cap you always wear?" Lora asked.

Scotty gasped.

"How did your cap get back here?" Lora asked him, puzzled.

"I don't know," he said, overwhelmed by a sudden feeling of dread.

He held back while she ran to get the cap.

"Lora? Wait!" he called.

But he was too late.

She bent over to pick up the cap, looked inside it, then, raising her hands to her face, started to scream.

# Chapter 16

"What is it?" Scotty cried, running over to her, his heart pounding.

"It — it's Fluffernutter!" she wailed.

Scotty put an arm around Lora's heaving shoulders and stared into the cap. The white cat was dead, its blue eyes already sunken back in a gruesome, glassy stare. Its body had been bent and stuffed tightly into the baseball cap.

"Who did this?" Lora wailed, tears pouring down her cheeks. "Who did this?"

Scotty stood gaping at her. Lora had always seemed to be in complete control. He had never seen her cry before.

"Fluffernutter!" she cried. She picked up the baseball cap and cradled it against her chest. "Poor Fluffernutter."

Shannon did this, Scotty realized.

I left the cap at her house. She never returned it.

Until now.

She'll do *anything*, he realized. *Anything*. She doesn't care what she kills or who she hurts.

He stared at the cast on his hand. First Shannon took out her jealousy on me. And now she has taken it out on Lora.

What am I going to do? What *can* I do?

I've go to stop Shannon. But how?

"Who did this?" Lora demanded, staring at him now, still cradling the dead cat in her arms. "Who?"

"I don't know," Scotty said softly, his arm around her tenderly. "I just can't imagine. . . ."

How long can I keep lying to Lora? he asked himself.

How many more horrors is Shannon going to commit before I'm forced to tell Lora the truth?

"Who did this? Who did this?" Lora repeated, holding the cat tightly, closing her eyes. Then she opened them and stared at Scotty, her expression hardening. "How did Fluffernutter get in your cap? How did your cap get in my backyard?"

"I don't know," Scotty lied. "I haven't seen the cap for days. I lost it over a week ago."

"You lost it?"

"Yeah. I've been looking and looking for it," he said. "I think maybe I must've left it at your house sometime."

"Poor Fluffernutter," Lora said, wet tears covering her eyes again. "I just don't understand this." She stared hard at Scotty, as if expecting him to have an answer.

He gently took the cap with its twisted corpse out

of her hands and set it back down on the ground.

I've got to tell her the truth, he decided.

I've got to stop lying. I just can't take this anymore.

I'll tell her about Shannon. Lora will be hurt and upset, but she'll forgive me. And once she knows the truth, we can both go to the police. We can stop Shannon once and for all.

Scotty took a deep breath. "Lora — I have to tell you — "

But before he could say another word, a large, dark figure stepped up from behind and grabbed Scotty by the shoulder.

# Chapter 17

Scotty spun around in terror.

"Mr. DeMarco!" he cried.

Lora's father grinned at him, squeezing his shoulder. "Sorry if I startled you. How is my favorite couple today?" He was wearing a smartly tailored, black wool suit, already dressed for the afternoon affair.

"Daddy — Fluffernutter is dead!" Lora wailed, pointing down to the cap on the ground. "Somebody killed her!"

Mr. DeMarco's broad smile shrank to an open-mouthed look of shock, and his normally ruddy face paled. He let go of Scotty's shoulder as he saw the contents of the cap.

He didn't say anything. His mouth froze in an O of surprise and puzzlement. He leaned his head down to examine the cat, then looked up at Scotty. "Isn't that your cap?"

Scotty felt his face grow red. "Yes," he muttered. "It's been lost for days,"

"How strange," Mr. DeMarco said, tucking his necktie back under his suit jacket with a trembling hand. "How strange."

It isn't strange at all, Scotty thought guiltily.

I could explain it to you in less than a minute.

But the desire to explain, to tell the truth, had left him. He knew he couldn't face both Lora and Mr. DeMarco together. They would be so disappointed in him. So hurt by his betrayal.

Things would never be the same again, Scotty realized.

Silently, he walked back to the house with them. The walk took only a few minutes, but it seemed like an eternity.


The Junior Chamber of Commerce Autumn Ball was held in the ballroom of the Sheraton. The room was vast, with rows of crystal chandeliers suspended from the high ceilings over the dozens of round, white tableclothed banquet tables spread over the room. There were tall flower arrangements as a centerpiece on every table. A large parquet dance floor stood to the right of the tables. In the front of the room, beyond the table of honor, stood a low stage where the dinner-jacketed orchestra sat.

Scotty immediately saw that he and Lora were just about the only young people in the room. They arrived a little after two to find the place already crowded, the orchestra already playing some lilting elevator music, waiters passing through the room with silver trays of hors d'oeuvres, a long line at the punch bowl.

Scotty's mother had her platinum hair piled high on her head and moussed until it stood as stiff as a sculpture. She wore her new chartreuse cocktail dress, the brightest dress in the room. But Scotty didn't mind. He was used to his mother's flamboyant style. Actually, he realized, the clothes she wore and her platinum hair were the only flamboyant things about her.

Mr. and Mrs. DeMarco were somewhat somberly dressed, especially in comparison with Mrs. Singleton. Mr. DeMarco wore his black wool suit with a dark, narrow tie. Mrs. DeMarco had chosen a tailored gray suit, the color just a shade darker than her graying hair, with a high-collared white blouse, offset by a dark blue silk scarf worn loosely as a tie around her neck.

Lora actually looked sensational in the blue sheath dress she had made fun of that morning. It had seemed dowdy and old-fashioned when she held it up in her room. But on her, Scotty thought, it became a very sexy party dress.

But of course, none of them were in a party mood this afternoon.

Mr. DeMarco had buried Fluffernutter by the fence in the backyard. Scotty's Raiders cap had been thrown into the trash.

They had all come to the hotel together in Mr. DeMarco's BMW. Mr. DeMarco had tried to cheer everyone up by telling funny stories he had heard at work. But, still thinking about the murdered cat in the backyard, they were a pretty grim crowd.

Now they entered the ballroom with forced smiles. The adults hurried to greet friends, shaking hands, kissing cheeks. Scotty and Lora got in line for some punch, both of them feeling tense and uncomfortable.

Scotty had dreaded this afternoon for weeks. He knew it would be boring and difficult, keeping a smile plastered to his face for hours as people, mostly friends of the DeMarcos, congratulated Lora and him, slapped him on the back, and told them what a good-looking couple they made and how proud everyone was of them.

But after what had happened, it was even harder than Scotty had imagined to keep it together. He didn't feel like smiling at these people, like making small talk about the warm winter they'd had so far, about school, and about the Tigers and what a shame it was that Scotty had broken his hand and couldn't finish the season.

Knowing how his hand had been broken, knowing how Lora's poor cat had been killed — knowing that he himself was largely responsible for the terrible things that were happening — was driving Scotty over the edge.

He felt like tearing off his stupid, plaid sports

jacket and the necktie that was choking him and tossing them in the trash. Then he'd run out the door and keep running.

Away from Lora. Away from the DeMarcos, even though they'd been so nice, so giving. Away from his mother. Away from Glenview. Away from everyone he knew.

Away from . . . Shannon.

He'd run and run and never stop.

"What are you thinking about?" Lora asked, filling a cup of the dark purple punch for him and handing him the glass cup, some of the liquid spilling over the sides.

"I'm thinking about how great you look in that dress," he lied. He spilled a little of the punch back into the gigantic crystal punch bowl.

She forced a smile. "And I'm thinking how that jacket *still* looks like a horse blanket!"

He laughed, pleased to see her smile again. They headed toward a corner, away from the dance floor crowded with people talking and laughing, where they could drink the awful, sweet punch in quiet.

But there was no escape today.

"Kids! Kids!" cried an excited woman's voice, and Mrs. Benedict, the president of the Junior Chamber of Commerce and organizer of this event, came hurrying over. She was a tall woman, as thin as a rail, dressed in a straight, black skirt that emphasized her slimness. She wore four or five huge, sparkling rings on her fingers and had at least six strands of gold and emerald beads around her neck, which clattered noisily as she came running up to them.

"Oh, we're all so excited!" she gushed, beaming at them both. "You two look wonderful."

Lora thanked her. Scotty nodded, nervously straightening his light brown hair with one hand.

"We're going to have lunch. Then I'm going to present your awards to you," Mrs. Benedict said. "And the check, of course," she added, and laughed a high-pitched laugh.

"Thank you," Lora said. Scotty repeated her words, shifting his weight uncomfortably, staring down at his empty punch cup.

"We're all so proud of both of you," Mrs. Benedict said. "You're both just so exceptional. And I understand you're both going to Princeton next fall. How wonderful!" She stopped. And blinked. "I'm embarrassing you, aren't I," she said in a subdued voice.

"No, not at all," Lora said quickly.

"Everyone's being so nice to us," Scotty added.

"I didn't mean to make you uncomfortable," Mrs. Benedict said. "I know this must be hard for you. My son Tim — you know Tim — well, he refused to come today. He's home playing Nintendo or goofing off. I'm sure you'd rather be doing that, too. It's just so refreshing to meet two truly *nice* young people these days."

"Thanks," Lora and Scotty said. They both shook hands with Mrs. Benedict, and she walked away, her necklaces clinking.

"She's not so bad," Lora said, watching her stop to greet some late arrivals.

"Her son's a total nerd," Scotty said, snickering.

"I don't think anyone wearing that sports jacket should call anyone else a total nerd," Lora cracked, "And what about that tie? Is that a clip-on?"

Scotty made an unhappy face, but he was secretly pleased that Lora was making jokes again. "Save my place against the wall here, okay?" he asked, handing her his empty punch cup.

"Where are you going? Are you ducking out?" she asked suspiciously.

"No," he told her. "I'm going to the bathroom. We can't be together *every* second, you know."

She stuck her tongue out at him. He rolled his eyes and started off across the room.

"Hey — what happened to your hand?" a middle-aged man in a red blazer asked as Scotty passed.

"Hunting accident," Scotty replied. He didn't know why he said that. The words just came to him. He decided he was starting to feel a little better, too.

He was making his way past the rows of tables when a young man he recognized as a cousin of the DeMarcos came hurrying up to him, a concerned look on his face. "Hey, Scotty!" he called.

Scotty tried to remember his name. "You're Paul, right?"

"Right," the young man said, not smiling. "I think you should go out front."

"Huh?" Scotty wasn't sure he heard him correctly.

"I think you're needed out front," Paul repeated, his forehead wrinkled with concern. "There's someone out there. A girl."

Scotty had a heavy, sinking feeling. "A girl? Out front? Why do they need me?"

"Well . . ." Paul reached a hand over his shoulder and rubbed the back of his neck. "Sorry. Stiff neck. I woke up with it."

"What about this girl?" Scotty demanded.

"She doesn't have an invitation, so they're not letting her in. But she says she's your date." Paul looked meaningfully across the room at Lora, who was still talking to her father.

"My date? That's totally bogus," Scotty said. "They should just send her away. I don't know who it could be." He lowered his voice confidentially to Paul. "Why would anyone want to crash *this* party?" He laughed.

Paul didn't seem to catch his humor. "Well, the lunch is going to be really fabulous," he replied, studying Scotty's face. "You'd better go out front. The hotel people are waiting for you, Scotty."

"Okay," Scotty said, realizing he had no choice. He could feel all of his muscles tense as he turned and walked to the ballroom doorway. He could hear his mother calling him from somewhere near the stage, but he just kept walking, taking long, steady strides.

What am I going to do? he thought, trying to fight down the panic he felt.

What am I going to say to Shannon? How can I get rid of her before anyone sees her?

A gong rang behind him in the ballroom. He heard chairs being scraped across the floor. Lunch was being served. He had felt hungry a few moments before, but now his stomach was tied in a knot.

He stepped out into the hallway. Two uniformed hotel workers, serious-looking young men with slicked-back black hair and hard expressions, were standing beside a wooden desk that had been set up to check off guests on the list as they arrived.

And there was Shannon. Standing between them, her arms crossed over her chest.

Scotty stopped at the doorway and stared at her.

What did she think she was doing? How did she have the nerve to come here?

Her hair had been carefully brushed for once, he saw, and tied back with a red hair ribbon. She was wearing a bright red dress, very tight, cut low in the front, very short, ending only halfway down her thighs.

She unfolded her arms to gesture at the two hotel guards, and Scotty saw that she was wearing short, red gloves that matched her dress.

Is that her idea of dressing up? Scotty thought. He was no fashion expert, but he knew that Shannon didn't look right for *this* place!

She looked so . . . tacky. Why had he ever thought

she was neat-looking? What had he seen in her?

He cleared his throat nervously and started toward her.

She saw him while he was still halfway across the lobby and called to him. "Scotty — here I am!"

"Shannon — what are you doing here?" he asked coldly, stepping up to the desk. One of the guards kept Shannon back, holding her by the arm.

"Tell them who I am, baby. They don't believe me," she said in her little-girl voice, making her eyes real big.

"She doesn't have an invitation, sir," the guard said, letting go of Shannon's arm. "Is she with you?"

"I'm your date, right, Scotty?" Shannon asked before Scotty could reply to the guard.

Scotty stared at her. "Shannon, I can't believe you're doing this," he said, his heart pounding but his voice low and steady.

"Tell them, Scotty," she said, smiling at him, ignoring his words. Her lips were covered with bright red lipstick. Some of it had smeared onto her front teeth.

"Why, Shannon?" Scotty asked, more of a plea than a question. "Why are you here?" He glanced back to the ballroom entrance, hoping no one was coming to look for him.

"I'm your date, baby," she insisted in her tiniest voice. "Tell them." Her voice remained tiny, but her eyes narrowed and her expression grew hard.

She pulled away from the guards and latched her arm around his.

"Sir, is she with you or not?" the guard asked impatiently.

"Tell them, baby," she said, pulling him toward the ballroom doors, her face hard, determined. "I'm your date. I'm coming in. I want to meet everybody."

# Chapter 18

"No," Scotty cried, trying to disentangle himself from her. "You can't!"

"I'm going in with you, Scotty." She clung to his arm, holding him tightly, staring up at him, her dark-lipsticked mouth set in a stubborn pout.

My life will be ruined, he thought, feeling himself overcome with panic. If I walk into the ballroom with her, if Lora sees me with her, if everyone sees her — my life will be ruined.

That's what Shannon wants. She wants to ruin my life.

"No!" he cried again, and pulled himself free of her grasp.

"Miss — " one of the hotel guards called, stepping around the desk, an alarmed look on his face.

"Stop, Miss," the other one called, looking suspiciously at Scotty.

"I'm your date. I'm going in there!" Shannon screamed. Her dark eyes flared angrily. Then she spun away from him and started to run across the lobby toward the ballroom, moving awkwardly in her red high-heeled pumps.

"Stop her!" Scotty pleaded.

She's going to humiliate me, he thought. She's going to humiliate me in front of everyone I care about.

He hesitated only a second. Then, seeing that the two guards were frozen in indecision, he took off after her.

She turned her head back as she ran and saw him coming. "I'm going in!" she yelled.

"No!" He leaped after her, and, ignoring the cast on his hand, made a diving tackle.

"Let go!" she shrieked.

His arm circled her waist. The force of his dive sent them both sprawling to the lobby carpet.

"Aaaiii!" he screamed in pain as she landed on his cast.

Heads turned. A woman across the lobby gasped. The two guards were moving fast toward Scotty.

"Let go! Let go! Let go!" Ignoring the pain shooting up his arm, he pulled himself up and forced her down onto her back. She swung her fists up at him. But he had her securely pinned on the floor.

Crying out, she reached up and pulled his necktie hard, choking him. As he struggled to loosen the tie with one good hand, she pulled herself out from under him, shoved him hard, and rolled on top of him.

This can't be happening, Scotty thought, looking up to see a horrified crowd around them. The two guards were bent over them, trying to pull Shannon off him.

"I'm going in!" she shouted, as the guard lifted her up by the arms. "I'm going in!" Her hair had come loose from the ribbon and was flying wildly about her face.

"What's going on here?" an important-looking man in a dark blue suit cried, breaking through the circle of onlookers.

"I'm going in," Shannon insisted, as the two guards struggled to pull her to the front exit.

Somewhat dazed, Scotty climbed to his feet. He touched his cheek. It felt wet. Looking at his hand, he realized his face was bleeding. Shannon must have scratched him as they scuffled.

Trying to catch his breath, he glanced toward the ballroom. Luckily no one had come out to witness the embarrassing scene. He looked around the crowd in the lobby and didn't recognize anyone.

"Are you okay?" the man in the dark suit asked.

"Yeah. I think so," Scotty said, holding his cheek. The hand under the cast throbbed with pain.

Shannon was being pulled, struggling and screaming, out of the lobby. People gasped and moved quickly out of the way as the two guards, one on each side, tried to remover her.

I've got to get back inside, Scotty thought, feeling a little relieved. Lora must be wondering where I am.

First, I've got to find a men's room and wash off this blood.

Then he gasped as he saw Shannon kick one of the guards hard in the knee. The guard cried out in pain and dropped to the floor.

With a burst of speed, Shannon broke away from the other startled guard, and came running back toward Scotty, heading to the ballroom.

"I'm your date, Scotty!" she yelled, staring at him, her eyes wild and frantic as she passed him, running awkwardly in the bulky high heels. "I'm your date! You can't keep me out!"

"Shannon — stop!" he yelled. He grabbed her again with his one good hand, and held on tight.

"Young man, I — I cannot allow this," the man in the blue suit sputtered. "You and your girlfriend must leave at once."

"But I'm going in," Shannon insisted.

"Shannon — please," Scotty begged, holding on desperately to her arm.

Suddenly, she stopped struggling. She looked up at him with her little-girl face and brushed his bleeding cheek tenderly with her gloved hand. "Tell them I'm your date, Scotty."

"Young man, I must insist — " the important-looking man, obviously the hotel manager, said.

An idea flashed into Scotty's mind, an idea born of panic, of desperation.

"Shannon — if I take you out next weekend, will you go home now?" he asked, not loosening his grip on her arm.

"You're hurting me," she cried, staring into his eyes.

Reluctantly he let go of her arm. "How about it, Shannon? Please? I'll take you out Saturday night. I promise."

"Really?" she asked in her tiny voice. "Just you and me?"

"Yes. Just you and me," he said quickly, seeing that she was considering it. "You go home now, and I promise I'll take you out next weekend."

"You promise?"

"I promise."

"Hope to die?" she asked.

Something about the way she said that gave him a chill. "I promise," he repeated, still breathing heavily, his chest heaving, his heart pounding. "Please, Shannon. Go home, okay? And Saturday night will be our night."

She stared up at him for a long moment, pulling loose strands of hair away from her face, "Okay," she said finally.

He breathed a loud sigh of relief, then bent down and picked up her red hair ribbon from the floor. "Good," he said softly, handing it to her.

He looked back toward the ballroom. No one had come out. He could hear voices and the clink of dishes and glasses. They must be halfway through lunch, he thought.

"Walk me to the door?" Shannon asked, pulling the red ribbon back and forth through her hand.

"Okay," Scotty quickly agreed.

*Anything* to get her out of here!

What am I going to tell Lora?

He felt his cheek. The bleeding seemed to have slowed. Some dark, dried blood flaked off on his fingers.

"I didn't mean to hurt you, baby," Shannon said softly.

"It's okay," he replied, leading her quickly to the door. People were staring at them from all over the huge lobby.

"You'll come to my house Saturday night?"

He pushed open the glass door and guided her out of the building. "Promise," he said.

The sky was overcast with dark clouds hovering low. It looked as if it might snow. The sudden cold made the cut on his face sting.

She looked up at him one more time as if trying to read in his face whether or not he was telling the truth. Then, without saying another word, she turned and began running along the walk that led past the hotel parking lot, her clunky red shoes clicking over the pavement.

What have I done? he thought. And then: What am I going to do?

He watched her as she passed the parking lot, running so awkwardly, not looking back. And then he saw the figure step out from behind a parked car in the main drive.

It was Shannon's brother. Scotty recognized him immediately even though he had never clearly seen his face. He recognized him from his enormous size and from his long raincoat.

The man was moving quickly toward Scotty,

pointing at him, calling to him even though he was too far away for Scotty to make out the words.

Does her brother follow her everywhere? Scotty wondered. What does he want?

Scotty had no intention of waiting to find out. He spun around, pulled open the door, and nearly knocking over an elderly couple who were trying to exit, bounded back into the hotel.

He won't follow me into the ballroom, Scotty decided. Taking long, quick strides, he headed across the lobby and down the hall toward the ballroom in back.

He was nearly there when he remembered that his face was cut. Looking down, he saw that his shirt had come untucked during his wrestling match with Shannon, the white flaps hanging down over his pants. A button had been torn off his sports jacket. His tie hung loose and crooked.

What should he do now?

Behind him, he saw Shannon's brother lumber into the lobby, looking in all directions, obviously searching for Scotty.

The ballroom offered safety. But Scotty knew he couldn't go back in there looking the way he did. He had to get himself cleaned up a bit first.

Praying that the hulking figure hadn't spotted him, Scotty ducked into the men's room, pulling the door closed behind him. He looked for a door lock, but there was none.

Moving to the mirrors over the row of sinks, he examined himself. The cut wasn't as bad as he had feared. It was just a scratch, actually. He picked up some paper towels from beside the sink, wet them, and dabbed the dried blood away.

Unfortunately, he had bled onto his shirt collar. He tried dabbing at the stain with the wet paper towel, but it only smeared the blood, making a larger stain.

He combed his hair, surprised that his hands were still trembling. Then he tucked in his shirt and retied his tie.

I don't look too bad, he thought.

Maybe I can go back in and pretend nothing happened.

And then, in the mirror, he saw the men's room door open and Shannon's brother step in.

# Chapter 19

Gaping into the mirror, Scotty hesitated for only a second.

As the big man moved through the narrow corridor that led to the sinks, Scotty darted to the stalls. He leaped into the nearest one and pulled the stall door closed, latching it silently.

Did he see me?

Does he know I'm in here?

His heart pounding, Scotty climbed up onto the toilet, hunched on the seat, keeping his feet off the floor so they couldn't be seen in the space beneath the stall door.

His chest felt tight. He had a strong urge to cough. His fright was making it hard to breathe.

Hunched on top of the toilet seat, he held his breath, forced himself not to cough . . . and listened.

The heavy footsteps against the marble floor grew louder. Closer.

Peering down beneath the stall door, Scotty could see the man's shadow on the floor. He was standing right in front of the stall.

He knows I'm here, Scotty thought, still holding

his breath even though it felt as if his lungs were about to burst. He knows.

He's standing there, waiting for me.

He's not going to make a move until I come out.

The shadow on the white tile floor shifted. Scotty could hear the man's shoes scrape as he moved.

Is he coming to get me? Scotty wondered, frozen in fear.

Is he going to force open the stall door, grab me, and pull me out?

The shadow on the floor seemed to freeze in place. Then, as Scotty stared down from his uncomfortable perch, it slid out of sight.

The shoes scraped heavily, moving away.

Scotty still didn't breathe, listening to the shoes move against the tile. When he heard the restroom door squeak open and then close, he exhaled loudly, but still didn't move.

He listened carefully.

Silence.

Struggling to catch his breath, he climbed down off the toilet seat. He unlatched the door, pulled it open, and stepped out.

Shannon's brother was waiting for him at the first sink. "Tricked you," he said, smiling. He had short blond hair, a round, red face with small gray eyes over a pudgy pug nose.

He took a step toward Scotty and pointed with two fingers. "I want to talk to you." He had a reedy, high-pitched voice, a voice much too small for a man of his size.

"I've got to g-go," Scotty managed to stammer. With a determined burst of speed, he ran toward Shannon's brother, then dodged away from him and scampered through the narrow corridor to the exit.

"Wait — " the brother cried, lurching toward Scotty.

But Scotty already had the restroom door open. He ran through it and across the lobby, past the two uniformed guards at the desk outside the ballroom door and into the ballroom.

Dessert was being served from pastry carts. Coffee was being poured from silver coffeepots. The room was quiet except for a few low murmurs.

Why isn't anyone talking? Scotty wondered, his eyes surveying the room. He quickly understood why. Mrs. Benedict was standing in the center of the main table, about to speak.

Forcing a smile to his face, hoping he looked at least a little normal, Scotty made his way through the tables to the front, being careful not to look at anyone. He didn't stop until he reached the table. Then he found his seat and slid in silently beside Lora.

She turned immediately and stared at him questioningly. "Scotty, where've you been?" she whispered. "You missed lunch."

"We're so proud of both of them," Mrs. Benedict was saying into the microphone standing just a few feet away, holding a stack of notecards in front of her. "Before I call them up to award them their prizes, let me tell you a little about these two young people and their accomplishments."

Lora continued to stare at him, searching his face. Suddenly, her eyes widened in surprise. "Scotty — you've been bleeding. What did you do to your face?" she whispered.

"I tripped," he whispered. "In the men's room. I fell onto the sink."

Her expression remained one of bewilderment. He wasn't sure whether she believed him or not.

"As you can see, both of them are citizens of the community as well as students," Mrs. Benedict was saying. She looked over at Scotty and Lora and blinked hard when she saw that they weren't paying attention to her speech.

"You're sweating like a pig," Lora whispered loudly. "Scotty, are you okay?"

I'll *never* be okay, Scotty thought glumly.

Never.

Not as long as Shannon is around.

She's never going to leave me alone. She's never going to quit.

All of my plans, all of my hopes — my whole life — it's all ruined.

"I'm going to to call Scotty and Lora up now, so let's give them a warm round of applause," Mrs. Benedict said.

# Chapter 20

Scotty called Lora Wednesday night. He had carefully rehearsed what he was going to say, but he was very nervous, uncertain of how she would react.

The phone rang once, and he dropped the receiver. Doing everything with one hand was really difficult, he had discovered. The big cast had been removed on Tuesday, replaced by one that was smaller but just as clunky.

He fumbled around on the floor of his room for the receiver. When he managed to return it to his ear, Lora was already on the other end. "Hello? Hello?"

"Hi, it's me," he said.

"Scotty, have you been avoiding me?" she asked.

"Huh? What are you talking about?"

Did she suspect something about Shannon?

"I haven't seen you since Saturday afternoon," Lora said.

"Yeah. I know," he said. "I've been studying and stuff."

"You've been kind of weird lately," she said. "I mean, weirder than usual."

"Is that a compliment?" he joked.

"Is anything the matter?" she asked.

What a question!

"No," he said. "Not really." There was an awkward silence, and then he began his prepared speech. "Lora, would it be okay if we don't go out Saturday night?"

"What?" The question seemed to take her by surprise.

"You see, my cousin is sick up in Meritville, and I thought I'd drive up and see him Saturday night."

"I thought you didn't have a car," she said suspiciously.

"Mom got a loaner from the insurance company. A Ford Taurus. It's actually much better than our car," he said.

"But can you drive with one hand?" she asked.

She suspects something, he thought. That's why she's asking so many questions.

"Yeah. No problem," he said. "I know we usually go out on Saturdays, but Eddie has always been a real pal and — "

"Scotty, I think you're confused," she said, suddenly sounding very cross.

"What?"

This wasn't going right, he realized. She was supposed to be sympathetic. She was supposed to tell him it was perfectly all right for him to go visit his sick cousin.

"How could you forget your own birthday?" she cried.

"Huh?"

"You can't visit your cousin on Saturday night, Scotty. That's the night we're celebrating your birthday, remember? I've made big plans. I'm picking you up at your house at nine and taking you someplace very special." She paused and then added sharply, "Doesn't *any* of this ring a bell?"

"Oh. Yeah," he said.

How could he have forgotten his own birthday? Lora had made such a fuss about how she was going to plan something really neat.

Oh, well, he thought, sighing. Lora isn't picking me up till nine. That'll give me time to get over to Shannon's early. I'll talk with Shannon, tell her I can't ever see her again, get everything straight with her once and for all, and be back at my house by nine.

"I feel like a total dork," he told Lora. "I — I just wasn't thinking clearly. Forget everything I said. I'll go visit my cousin on Sunday."

"That's better," she said. But she still sounded very suspicious.

"Uh . . . Lora?"

He had this sudden urge to tell her how sorry he was. He wanted to tell her that he hadn't meant to mess everything up. He wanted to tell her that Shannon didn't mean anything to him, that he didn't even like Shannon, that she was a mistake, a horrible mistake that he had regretted from the first night he had met her.

He felt like telling Lora everything, just letting it all spill out. Not to cleanse himself. Not to make himself feel better. But just to let Lora know that he didn't like having to lie to her, that he didn't like what Shannon had forced him to become.

"Yes?" Lora asked, a little impatiently.

"I just want you to know I care about you," he said. His throat tightened. He couldn't say more.

"Me, too," she said quickly.

"No matter what happens," he added.

"What?" she cried. "What do you mean? Scotty?"

"I'll call you," he said and gently hung up the phone.

# Chapter 21

Saturday was gray and cold. A sharp wind blew down from the north, toppling garbage cans, sweeping the fallen dead leaves over the front yard like a crackling, brown river. The sun never appeared, and by late afternoon it was as dark as midnight.

Scotty didn't notice the wind or the cold as he climbed into the white Taurus a little after six o'clock to drive to Shannon's house. Thinking about her, about all she had done, about all she *could* do to ruin his life, he had felt edgy all day. But now, as he backed down the drive and headed toward the Old Village, his nervousness gave way to anger.

He had had only one date with Shannon. He had made no promises to her. He hadn't misled her in any way. What right did she have to keep pestering him, to follow him, to call him constantly, to try to invade his life?

She had no right. No right at all.

His mind whirled as he repeated over and over the things he planned to say to her. All of his attempts to get through to her, to make her stop, to get rid of her, had failed.

But not tonight, he told himself. Not tonight.

Tonight would be different. Tonight he would *make* her understand. Tonight he would make her *promise* to leave him alone.

And if she didn't agree?

He would talk to her parents. Or her brothers. He would tell them how unbalanced Shannon was. How dangerous.

Dangerous.

Well, Scotty thought, I can be dangerous, too.

I can get tough if I have to.

Distracted by his angry thoughts, he sped through a stop sign. The squeal of another car's brakes alerted him to what he had done, but he didn't look back.

I'm going to make this short, he told himself, glancing down at the digital clock on the dashboard. Six-twenty.

He knew he had to be back home by nine, when Lora planned to pick him up.

No problem, he thought.

As he drove into Shannon's neighborhood, the houses passing by in the darkness were smaller and closer together. A burst of wind shook the car. He gripped the wheel tighter with his left hand, his other hand resting uselessly on his lap.

Halfway down the block, he squealed to a stop. He had driven right past Shannon's house. Cursing to himself, he threw the car into reverse and backed up along the curb. He parked at the bottom of her dirt driveway. Then he cut the engine and climbed out, slamming the door behind him.

The house was dark except for a dim yellow light glowing behind the lowered window shade in the front window. Scotty jogged up the drive, ducking his head against the strong wind.

Why did I ever come here? he thought.

Why did I ever get involved with her?

He couldn't decide if he was more angry at Shannon or at himself. His temples throbbed as he climbed the two steps of her front stoop. He felt strange, out of control, angry, and nervous — and a little frightened.

Taking a deep breath, he raised his hand to knock on the front door, and it was pulled open.

Shannon stood in the pale yellow light. She was dressed all in white, in a short, straight skirt and a white turtleneck sweatertop. Her red hair shone in the light, falling softly down in front of her shoulders.

She smiled at him, her dark eyes lighting up.

She looks like a little angel, Scotty thought.

What a joke.

"Hi, baby. You're late," she said softly.

Stepping into the small front room, he didn't return her smile. "Hi," he said, keeping his expression hard.

"Let me hang up your coat," she said, reaching up to help pull off his down jacket.

"No. I'm not staying long," he said sharply, looking around at the threadbare furniture, the peeling wallpaper, the bare floorboards. "Are your parents home? Or your brothers?"

She gave him a devilish look. "No, baby. Don't worry. No one's home. We're all alone." She took his jacket and hung it up in the front closet.

She smelled sweet and flowery. He realized she was wearing a lot of perfume.

"Please don't call me baby," he said sharply.

When she turned around, she had a slightly mocking expression on her face. "Why not, baby?" she asked in her whispery voice.

"Because I'm *not* your baby!" he shouted.

She put her hand gently on his shoulder. "I made you a special dinner. Because this is such a special night."

He stared at her, surprised. "You cooked dinner?"

"Yes. Just for the two of us. Look." She pointed to a small table in the adjoining room. It had been set for two. A single candle glimmered in the center. "Surprised?"

"Shannon, I'm sorry. I'm not going to stay," Scotty said. He struggled to remember what he had planned to say, what he had rehearsed over and over in his mind all week. But he was drawing a blank.

"Come sit down, Scotty," she said, taking his hand.

He pulled his hand away. "Didn't you hear me?"

"How's your hand?" she asked, studying the cast. "It doesn't hurt anymore, does it?"

"Shannon — don't ignore me," he said, feeling his anger rise.

"That was such a shame, such a nasty accident," she said, pushing her lipsticked mouth into a pout.

"It wasn't an accident," he said, glaring at her. "You did it deliberately."

"I wouldn't hurt you. You're my baby," she said softly. She reached up and grabbed the back of his head with both hands. Then she pulled his head down and pressed her lips against his.

She smelled so sweet. Her lips were so soft.

"*No!*" he screamed.

It was hard to pull away from her, especially with just one useful hand. She grasped the back of his head, holding him tightly. It was no longer a tender hold. It was violent, desperate.

Finally he managed to duck out of her grasp. He backed away, holding his hand up as if it were a shield. "Stop it, Shannon."

"But what's the matter? Don't you *like* me anymore?" Her voice sounded tiny and hurt.

"No," he said flatly.

She stared into his eyes. "You're not being nice to me, Scotty."

"I came here to say leave me alone," he said, staring right back at her. "Leave me alone, Shannon. Don't call me. Don't follow me. Don't come to see me."

"I made such a nice dinner for us," she said.

"I want you to leave me alone. And I want you to leave my friends alone," he continued.

"I want this night to be special," she said softly.

"Aren't you listening to me?" he screamed. He could feel himself losing it, but he didn't care.

He had to make her hear him.

He *had* to!

"Listen to me, Shannon. I'm leaving now. Right now. And I'm never coming back. Do you hear me?"

"Don't leave," she said, her face expressionless now. Her smile had faded; her eyes lost their sparkle. "I don't think you should leave."

"What are you going to do? Break my *other* hand?" he cried.

"No," she said softly, "If you leave, I'll do something worse."

"Worse?" His chest was heaving. He had never felt such anger, such frustration.

"I'll tell Lora," she said.

She waited for him to react, but he just glared at her.

"I'll tell Lora everything," Shannon said, her face a pale, cold mask, revealing no emotion at all. "I'll go see her. I'll tell her that you want to be with *me* now."

"No, you won't!" he screamed. "You won't!"

In a total rage, he grabbed her narrow shoulders and began to shake her.

The next few seconds became a noisy blur.

He suddenly felt as if he weren't here in this

shabby, dimly lit living room, as if he were somewhere above it, hovering over the room, watching
the boy and girl struggle beneath him.

It wasn't him shaking Shannon so violently. It
wasn't him roaring out his rage and frustration. It
wasn't him making her head snap back like that,
her long hair tossing wildly over her face, then behind her shoulders.

He wasn't doing it. He wasn't struggling with
her, pushing her, choking her, slamming her small
body against the dark wall.

"You've ruined my life! You've ruined my life!"

He wasn't crying out like that. He wasn't making
her cry out.

He was above it, outside it, away from them,
watching them.

And then suddenly the blur, the violent blur
cleared.

And he saw everything so clearly.

Shannon was on the floor, crumpled in such a
strange position, her head tilted at such a strange
angle, her white skirt up over her pale thighs.

Her eyes were closed.

He could see everything so clearly.

Her eyes were closed, and she wasn't breathing.

So clear. So clear.

He had killed her.

# Chapter 22

I didn't kill Shannon, he thought, staring down at her, his eyes focusing and unfocusing.

I didn't kill her.

I'm the quarterback. I was all-state last season.

I should've been all-state again *this* season.

I'm too young.

I hardly knew her.

So how could I have killed her?

Lora and I are the perfect couple. Everyone is so happy for us.

So happy.

I couldn't kill Shannon.

I've already been accepted at Princeton. Of course, I haven't heard from the scholarship people yet. But it's almost a sure thing.

Lora and I will be there together.

It seems we've always been together.

We belong together. We're the perfect couple.

So I couldn't have killed Shannon.

"Get up, Shannon!" he yelled. He nudged her side with the toe of his sneaker.

"Get up! Get up — please!"

He stood over her unmoving form. He couldn't bend down. He wanted to, but he couldn't move. He could only stand there.

Maybe I'm dead, too, he thought.

No. That's crazy. Crazy.

I'm the quarterback, Scotty Singleton.

I'm the perfect couple.

There's a place waiting for me at Mr. DeMarco's agency.

So I can't be dead. And neither can Shannon.

He could see everything so clearly, every detail in the room, every thread in Shannon's white cotton sweater, every hair on her head. Her hair was splayed out on the floor. Her legs were bent beneath her.

Lora and I are the couple of the year, he thought.

He tried to remember his little brother's name. Why couldn't he think of it?

I'm not thinking clearly, he realized, staring down at her hair, so tangled and wild.

I can see very clearly. But I'm not thinking clearly.

He turned and walked over to the worn couch. He dropped down onto it, closed his eyes, and rubbed the eyelids with the fingers of his good hand.

Denny. That's his name.

Okay. That's a little better.

He sat with his eyes closed for a long time, waiting for the panic to subside.

I'm just not thinking clearly. I've got to think clearly.

What do I do now?

She can't be dead. So what do I do now?

After all, I'm the quarterback.

Coach Hawkins is really going to chew me out about this.

I'm still not thinking clearly.

Denny. His name is Denny.

That's good. That's good for a start. But what do I *do* now?

He got up and walked back to her. "Aren't you going to move?" he asked softly. "Isn't dinner going to get cold?"

Aren't *you* going to get cold?

He had to do something to clear his head. He would never think clearly if he stood staring down at her, waiting for her to move.

He would never get his scholarship.

He would never pass Go and collect two hundred dollars.

I've got to get out of here, he realized.

I've got to go somewhere and think. I'm not thinking clearly here. If I go away, I'll be able to figure everything out.

And then I'll go to Princeton. With Lora.

I'll call Lora right now. We can go to Princeton tonight.

No. He wasn't thinking clearly. Lora wasn't home.

She wasn't home.

An idea flashed into his spinning head. Even in the confusion, he knew he could figure out what to do if he got out of that house. He knew the cold air would help clear his head. Getting away from her body would help drive away his panic.

Her body?

Why did he think of her as a body now? She couldn't be dead.

He was too young.

And he was very smart. All the tests showed it.

He moved quickly to the front closet, grabbed his coat, and struggled into it, pulling it over his broken hand first, then easing his good hand through the other sleeve.

I'm not thinking clearly. I'm just not thinking clearly.

He searched the jacket pocket until he found the car keys. Then he pulled open the front door and started out.

A strong gust of wind blew him back.

I'm not thinking clearly. I've got to get away, go somewhere quiet, somewhere peaceful to think.

But I can't leave Shannon here.

She's not dead. But what if her parents come home? What if they find her lying on the floor, all twisted like that? They might *think* she's dead.

And I could get in trouble. Bad trouble.

Or what if her brothers come home? They could make a mistake, too. They could think she's dead. And then they'd come after me. Like that one huge brother of hers.

I'm not thinking clearly.

I'd better take her with me. Yes. I'll take her with me. And when I'm feeling a little better, a little calmer, a little quieter, I'll know what to do.

Picking Shannon up was hard, especially with only one good hand. Slinging her over his shoulder was even harder.

Luckily she was small and light.

Not as light as a feather, he thought. But light enough to carry out to the car.

She still felt warm as he draped her over his shoulder, holding her around the back of her legs with one arm. He made his way unsteadily to the front door, thought about getting her a coat, but decided he couldn't put her down again.

Out into the blustery wind. The front yard was dark. There was no porch light. The neighbors couldn't see him.

She started to get heavier as he carried her down the dirt drive. She was slipping off his shoulder.

Just a few more feet, he thought. The wind seemed to be blowing at him from all directions at once, making it hard to move forward, and hard to balance this heavy, sprawling weight.

He was breathing hard by the time he reached the car. Bending down, her arms dangling in front of him, he pulled open the back door. Then he bent lower until she was even with the seat, and he lurched forward, letting her go tumbling off his shoulders and onto the car seat.

She landed facedown. He waited, expecting her to pick herself up. But she didn't move.

He pushed the rest of her onto the seat, straightened her skirt, and tucked her legs in. Slamming the door shut, he leaned against the car, gasping for air, struggling to catch his breath, his shoulders aching, his broken hand throbbing all the way up the arm.

Where shall I go?

Got to think. Got to think.

Lora isn't home. The words flashed into his mind again.

Lora isn't home. She's picking me up at my house.

So he'd take Shannon to Lora's house. The back door was always unlocked. He'd hide her down in the cellar. Just for a short while. Just long enough for him to start thinking clearly again.

Having this plan made him feel a little better. He stepped away from the car and started to walk around it to the driver's side. He opened the car door, but dropped the keys onto the street.

He found them easily, then climbed behind the wheel.

"Are you still back there?" he called, struggling to slip the key into the ignition with his trembling hand.

No answer.

"Did you buckle up?" he asked.

Again no answer.

He glanced at her in the rearview mirror. She still lay facedown, her hair splayed out at odd angles all around her head.

"I know you're breathing," he called back to her. "I'm just not thinking clearly."

But that would change as soon as he dropped her off at Lora's. He'd leave her in the basement, in the cedar closet in the rec room. Then he'd go somewhere quiet and think.

The drive to Lora's was another blur. There didn't seem to be much traffic on the road. Or maybe he just didn't see the other cars.

It seemed like an instantaneous trip to him. A second later, he had pulled the Taurus up the smooth, curving drive to the back of Lora's house.

The house was dark except for the outside lights, front and back. A spotlight above the middle door on the three-car garage shone in his eyes. He climbed out of the car to get away from it.

No one is home, he realized, peering into the back windows.

Breathing a sigh of relief, he opened the rear car door. Then he bent down and started to pull Shannon out of the car. It took a long time to get her back onto his shoulders. For some reason, she seemed much heavier now. By the time he reached the back door, he was breathing noisily, and bathed in perspiration.

His entire body ached. He shifted her on his

shoulders and reached for the doorknob. She was draped over his shoulders now, like a shawl, her arms dangling down to his right, her legs to his left.

He turned the knob. And breathed a sigh of relief as the door pushed open.

Yes. Unlocked as usual.

He stepped forward, but her arms and legs caught on the sides of the door. Backing up, he turned sideways and slipped into the dark kitchen.

It was warm inside, and smelled of baked apples.

For a long moment, he stood in the doorway, inhaling the sweet smell, waiting for his eyes to adjust to the dark, balancing Shannon on his shoulders.

I'm starting to feel better already, he thought.

Just being away from her house has helped.

Now I'll take her down to the basement and go figure out what to do.

He turned carefully to the wall and clicked on the kitchen light.

Then, balancing Shannon awkwardly, he turned around.

And as he turned, Lora, Bender, the DeMarcos, his mother, and about twenty or thirty other friends jumped up from behind the kitchen counters, all shouting in unison: "SURPRISE!"

# Chapter 23

"Happy birthday!" Lora cried, and then her eyes bulged and her mouth dropped open in horror as she saw the girl's body around his shoulders.

Scotty reeled back and stared into the crowd of familiar faces. Their smiles seemed to fade in slow motion as their expressions changed to horror and confusion.

Shannon slid off his shoulders and hit the linoleum floor with a soft thud. She groaned as she hit the floor and her eyes opened. "Huh?" she cried groggily.

"I knew she wasn't dead," Scotty said aloud.

The shock of seeing Lora and everyone was helping to snap his mind back to normal.

"Scotty — who is that? What's going on?" Mr. DeMarco demanded. He hurried over and knelt down beside Shannon, who was groaning loudly, lying on her back behind Scotty.

"It — it's hard to explain," Scotty said, feeling dizzy and weak.

Everything that had happened was coming back to him all at once. He was finally thinking clearly.

"I thought I killed her," he said.

There were loud gasps. Everyone started to talk at once.

Bender came over and put a hand on Scotty's shoulder. "I recognize her, man," he said quietly. "She's the one who did your hand."

"I really can't talk about it now," Scotty said, turning to watch Mr. DeMarco, who was still tending to Shannon.

"Scotty — who is she?" Lora demanded.

"I think I have to sit down," Scotty said weakly.

Her features drawn with worry and confusion, Lora took his arm and started to lead him out of the kitchen. The counter, Scotty noticed as they passed, was piled high with colorfully wrapped birthday presents.

"We didn't even have time to get the presents organized," Lora muttered. "How did you know we were here?"

"I didn't," Scotty said honestly. He decided he was going to be completely honest with her, completely honest from now on. He'd tell her everything, and pray that she'd forgive him.

She led him to the kitchen table and pulled out a chair for him. He dropped down onto it gratefully, his head spinning, the loud, excited voices echoing in his ears.

Across the room, Shannon was on her feet. Mr. DeMarco was holding her by the arm. She was tugging at her hair, pulling it behind her shoulders.

"Who is she?" Lora demanded, standing beside Scotty, staring across the room as Shannon talked to Mr. DeMarco and several others.

"She's a girl from our school," Scotty said quietly. "I met her at Homecoming, the night you were away. In Paris. I did a really bogus thing. I — I took her out while you were gone."

"You what?" Lora looked down at him in surprise.

"It's a long story," he said. "I feel really bad. I'm really sorry. But she — she's crazy, Lora. She wouldn't leave me alone. She killed Ernie, and she broke my hand. She killed your cat, too, and — "

He stopped his explanation and jumped to his feet, his eyes growing wide with fear.

Across the kitchen, Shannon had stepped away from Mr. DeMarco. As Scotty watched, she darted over to the pile of birthday presents, her eyes wild, her expression hard and determined. Without saying a word, she tore the blue and green ribbons off a pair of ski poles propped against the counter.

She grabbed a ski pole by the handle, letting its companion drop to the floor. Her eyes moved slowly around the room until they found Scotty.

"Whoa! Hold on!" Scotty heard Bender yell from somewhere across the kitchen.

Scotty stepped away from Lora and called to Shannon. "What are you doing?"

She didn't answer him. She glared at him with

pure hatred, and raised the pointed end of the ski pole toward him.

"You're not my baby anymore!" she screamed, her voice loud and raspy, unlike any sound he had ever heard from her before.

"Shannon, wait — " he cried.

But she came rushing at him, holding the ski pole like a sword.

"No!" he cried, frozen to the spot, realizing she meant to kill him.

Screaming at the top of her lungs, she lunged toward him.

He dodged, and the pointed ski pole slid a few inches past his side and rammed the wall with a loud *crack*. The handle flew out of Shannon's hand. But she quickly picked it up and came after Scotty again.

"No, Shannon — please!" He turned and ran across the kitchen. The back door was open. He heaved himself toward it, thinking only of escape.

And then stopped short.

Shannon's enormous brother stood on the other side, his face twisted in menace.

# Chapter 24

Scotty backed away from the door. "She's okay! I didn't kill her!" he screamed.

Behind him, Mr. DeMarco and several others were wrestling the ski pole from Shannon's hands. She was screaming and struggling to keep it away from them.

"Your sister is okay," Scotty repeated, his trembling voice revealing his fear as the big man pushed open the door and came toward him.

"Sister?" the man asked in his high-pitched voice. He stared at Scotty questioningly and reached into his pocket.

He's got a gun! Scotty thought, stumbling backwards.

"Look out — he's going to shoot!" Scotty screamed.

But the man pulled a small leather card holder out of his pocket and flipped it open, revealing a police badge. "Lieutenant Jarmusch, juvenile division," he said, and quickly replaced the badge.

Then he bounded across the room, moving very fast for someone of his size, and grabbed Shannon by both shoulders.

She stopped screaming and struggling. She seemed to recognize him. "Uh-oh," she said quietly, rolling her eyes.

"Is everyone okay?" Jarmusch asked, holding Shannon firmly, looking around at the startled faces. "This one can be dangerous," he said.

"Uh-oh," Shannon repeated, shaking her head. "Busted again."

"You — you're not her brother?" Scotty asked, his head still spinning.

"Brother?" The big police officer laughed, a high, wheezy laugh. "She doesn't have any brothers. No family at all, as far as I can tell." His expression changed. He looked accusingly at Scotty. "I've been trying to talk to you, son."

"I — I thought you were her brother," Scotty said, embarrassed.

"Uh-oh," Shannon said and laughed scornfully at Scotty.

"This one was sent up for manslaughter," Jarmusch said, holding tightly to Shannon's shoulders. "But she only did juvenile time. You know. Like ten minutes." He snickered, shaking his head.

"She's been seeing her parole officer regularly. Has her parole officer convinced that she's got her act together. But I had a hunch she was up to no good again. So I've been doing a little surveillance work on her in my spare time. Spare time? That's a joke."

"Uh-oh," Shannon muttered. "He made a joke."

"Just chill out," Jarmusch told Shannon. "It took me till yesterday to get a legal search warrant for her house. Just as I suspected, she's been lying to us about living with her mother. She's all alone in there. No family. Nobody. I've been trying to get enough hard evidence to show that she still needs help. I don't want her to do more time. I just want her to get the treatment she needs."

Shannon puckered her lips and, looking at Scotty, made loud kissing noises.

Scotty looked away.

Jarmusch did a little more explaining, told Scotty he'd need a statement from him tomorrow, then led Shannon away. She didn't resist, looking back longingly at Scotty for a long moment, then disappearing out the back door, followed by the bulky policeman.

"I think maybe we'd better postpone this birthday party," Mr. DeMarco announced when he was gone. "I think we're all too confused to feel like celebrating."

Scotty slumped at the kitchen table as everyone filed out, retrieving their coats from the front closet. His mother stopped to put a hand on his shoulder. "Are you coming home now?"

"Soon," Scotty said. "I want to talk to Lora first."

When everyone had left, Lora, sitting across the

white Formica table from Scotty, shook her head. "You sure know how to pick 'em," she said dryly.

He looked up at her guiltily. "Don't be angry at me, okay?"

She reached across the table and squeezed his hand. "Maybe we're just trying to do things too soon, you know." Her face grew serious. "We've been acting like an old, married couple since we were twelve. Maybe it's a mistake."

"I'm the only one who made a mistake," he said softly.

"We don't have to talk about it tonight," she said, still holding his hand. A smile slowly spread across her face. "I'm just angry that that girl spoiled my birthday present for you."

"Present? What present?" he asked.

"The ski poles, of course!"

They both laughed.

"What a birthday!" Scotty exclaimed.

"Well," said Lora thoughtfully, "I'll tell you one thing. This was one surprise party that was a *surprise* — for everyone!"

They were both still smiling as she walked him out to his car to say good night.

# About the Author

R. L. STINE is the author of over one hundred books of mystery, adventure, and humor for young people. In recent years, he has written more than twenty scary thrillers, nearly all of them best-sellers.

He is the author of the humorous SPACE CADETS book series. And, as Jovial Bob Stine, he has written many joke books. In addition to his publishing work, he is head writer of the TV series *Eureeka's Castle*, seen on *Nickelodeon*.

Bob lives in Manhattan with his wife, Jane, and his son, Matt.

# *point*®

## Other books you will enjoy,
## about real kids like you!

# *point* ® THRILLERS

## R.L. Stine

- ❏ MC44236-8 The Baby-sitter — $3.25
- ❏ MC44332-1 The Baby-sitter II — $3.25
- ❏ MC45386-6 Beach House — $3.25
- ❏ MC43278-8 Beach Party — $3.25
- ❏ MC43125-0 Blind Date — $3.25
- ❏ MC43279-6 The Boyfriend — $3.25
- ❏ MC44333-X The Girlfriend — $3.25
- ❏ MC45385-8 Hit and Run — $3.25
- ❏ MC43280-X The Snowman — $3.25
- ❏ MC43139-0 Twisted — $3.25

## Caroline B. Cooney

- ❏ MC44316-X The Cheerleader — $3.25
- ❏ MC41641-3 The Fire — $3.25
- ❏ MC43806-9 The Fog — $3.25
- ❏ MC45681-4 Freeze Tag (11/92) — $3.25
- ❏ MC45402-1 The Perfume — $3.25
- ❏ MC44884-6 Return of the Vampire — $2.95
- ❏ MC41640-5 The Snow — $3.25

## Diane Hoh

- ❏ MC44330-5 The Accident — $3.25
- ❏ MC45401-3 The Fever — $3.25
- ❏ MC43050-5 Funhouse — $3.25
- ❏ MC44904-4 The Invitation — $2.95
- ❏ MC45640-7 The Train (9/92) — $3.25

## Sinclair Smith

- ❏ MC45063-8 The Waitress — $2.95

## Christopher Pike

- ❏ MC43014-9 Slumber Party — $3.25
- ❏ MC44256-2 Weekend — $3.25

## A. Bates

- ❏ MC45829-9 The Dead Game (12/92) — $3.25
- ❏ MC43291-5 Final Exam — $3.25
- ❏ MC44582-0 Mother's Helper — $2.95
- ❏ MC44238-4 Party Line — $3.25

## D.E. Athkins

- ❏ MC45246-0 Mirror, Mirror — $3.25
- ❏ MC45349-1 The Ripper (10/92) — $3.25
- ❏ MC44941-9 Sister Dearest — $2.95

## Carol Ellis

- ❏ MC44768-8 My Secret Admirer — $3.25
- ❏ MC44916-8 The Window — $2.95

## Richie Tankersley Cusick

- ❏ MC43115-3 April Fools — $3.25
- ❏ MC43203-6 The Lifeguard — $3.25
- ❏ MC43114-5 Teacher's Pet — $3.25
- ❏ MC44235-X Trick or Treat — $3.25

## Lael Littke

- ❏ MC44237-6 Prom Dress — $3.25

## Edited by T. Pines

- ❏ MC45256-8 Thirteen — $3.50

---

Available wherever you buy books, or use this order form.

**Scholastic Inc., P.O. Box 7502, 2931 East McCarty Street, Jefferson City, MO 65102**

Please send me the books I have checked above. I am enclosing $_____ (please add $2.00 to cover shipping and handling). Send check or money order — no cash or C.O.D.s please.

Name _____

Address_____

City_____ State/Zip_____

Please allow four to six weeks for delivery. Offer good in the U.S. only. Sorry, mail orders are not available to residents of Canada. Prices subject to change.                    PT192